KANSAS CITY CHORINE

"Kick your pants off and walk backward," the gunman ordered. "And no tricks! Try anything and your guts'll be sizzling in the sunshine!"

Spur sighed. This wasn't his day. "What kind of man are you? You'd use your pretty wife to rob innocent men?"

The gunman snorted. "Elsie, go over there and do what you do best—get the man's pants off!"

The young woman smiled, walked to McCoy and bent over.

Spur flipped his left boot up into the air. He caught his gunbelt as it sailed up in front of him. McCoy simultaneously pulled the blonde to him and unholstered his Colt. A second later he had its muzzle pressed against the screaming woman's throat....

Also in the *Spur* Series:

SPUR #28

KANSAS CITY CHORINE

DIRK FLETCHER

LEISURE BOOKS NEW YORK CITY

A LEISURE BOOK®

September 2005

Published by

Dorchester Publishing Co., Inc.
200 Madison Avenue
New York, NY 10016

ISBN 0-8439-2714-3

The name "Leisure Books" and the stylized "L" with design are trademarks of Dorchester Publishing Co., Inc.

Printed in the United States of America.

Visit us on the web at www.dorchesterpub.com.

KANSAS CITY CHORINE

1

Don't want to blow myself up, Jack T. Galde thought as he walked through the town. Gingerly gripping the denim-wrapped bundle, he peered around the corner of Maple Street. No one in sight.

Galde quickly cleared the last forty yards and approached the hulking brick building from behind. The Forestville Bank had been built to withstand anything but dynamite, he mused, as he crouched near his predetermined spot.

A few faint peeps from the tree beside him startled the man. Just a bird waking up, he thought. Don't get all riled up, Galde! Everything will go fine. Nothing could go wrong now. You've planned too carefully.

Galde placed the bundle on the ground and unwrapped it. Five sticks. Should be enough, he mused.

The man worked quickly, sweating in the darkness. He stuck a blasting cap into one of the long, red tubes and attached five feet of fuse to it. That was just enough to reach behind the tree.

Satisfied by his handiwork, Galde nestled the bomb against the bank's left wall and trailed the fuse into the clump of small saplings, checking with his fingers through the darkness that nothing would impede the fuse's slow burn.

That finished, Galde returned to his hotel room. Excitement ripped through him as he silently climbed the stairs. He was doing it again. Another bank. Another load of money and gold. Another fast escape and another search for a new target.

It invigorated him, this game of hide and seek, these aliases and phony names, the way he'd work his way into some small town and then, when he was trusted, rob the bank, kill anyone who got in his way, and ride out of town.

Galde went into his room, closed the door and swallowed a mouthful of whiskey. In the dim light spilling from the kerosene wall lamp he smiled and raised the bottle to his lips again. No, he told himself. You don't want to get drunk. He returned it to the rickety table. Time enough for drinking later.

Galde checked the sky through the cracked window. Blue light tinged the eastern horizon beyond the livery stable. Sunrise wasn't far off and he was right on time.

Twenty minutes, the stocky man mused. He had twenty more minutes to wait.

Then he'd never have to face the simple-minded fools of Jacksonville again.

Smirking, he gave himself a whore's bath in the

cracked basin and used the hard lye soap. He then changed into his riding clothes and packed his old carpetbag. Dress for the occasion, he reminded himself.

At 5:20 Galde left his hotel room, lugging his saddlebags. He untied his horse from the hitching post in front of the hotel and rode her out of town 200 yards, then turned back and halted his mount behind the bank. No one should be going back there this time of morning. He tied the sleepy mare to an oak tree and grabbed his saddlebags.

Three minutes later he heard boots kicking through the dirt and keys jingling. Bud Ormond was arriving right on time. Pulling a red kerchief up around his face, Galde slipped down the far side of the bank and peered around the wall. The tall, blonde haired, hatless man struggled with the lock in the bank's front door.

"Damn!" he muttered.

Galde sidled up to him, silently drawing his six-gun. He pushed its muzzle against Ormond's back.

"What th—"

"Shut up!" Galde hissed. "Just open the door and walk in like nothing unusual's happening, unless you want me to blast your worthless guts all over the street, Ormond!"

"No. No!" The young man finally turned the cylinders and pushed open the door.

Galde shoved him inside the cool building, removed the key from the lock and quietly locked the door from the inside.

Ormond still stood facing away from him, his knees shaking.

"Turn around!" Galde growled.

The banker did, presenting a shadowy face.

"Listen up, Ormond. I want you to open the safe. Now!"

The man glanced around him. "But—but Mr. Drithers isn't here and I—"

"Look, Ormond, I ain't trying to make a deposit, just a withdrawal!" He motioned with his six-gun. "Move your ass before I blow you to bits!"

"Sure! Sure!" The thin man hustled to the rear of the bank, stumbled between the two oak desks and crouched next to the waist-high, iron safe.

"Hurry!" Galde growled as he followed him.

Ormond flipped the lock twice to clear it and began working out the combination. His fingers faltered.

"I'm—I'm sorry, I—" Ormond began.

"Just do it!"

He successfully entered all three numbers and pulled the handle. The heavy door swung open.

"Stand up and back towards me. And don't try nothing!"

"I—I won't." He moved toward Galde.

When he was four feet away, the bank robber grunted. "Far enough. Lay down with your head facing the left wall."

The man looked at him quizzically. "You—you ain't gonna kill me?" His face in the growing light was confused.

Galde smirked. "Not unless you try anything."

As the man got into the prescribed position, Galde bolted for the safe. He reached into it and pulled out three small bags. Testing their weight he knew they had to be filled with gold coins. He stuffed them into the saddlebags he'd carried with him. Two more searches with his hand revealed neatly stacked piles of ones, tens and twenties, along with two hundred-dollar bills.

Galde snarled as he emptied the safe into his saddlebags. Not much, but enough for a while. He closed the bag and stood upright.

"You—you finished now, mister?" Ormond asked.

"Yeah. Almost. Why?"

"Cause—cause I'm gonna piss my pants."

Galde laughed.

"Hey, I know who you are!" the banker said, looking over his shoulder. "You're Emil Jackson!"

"Get your ugly face back on the floor!" Galde yelled.

The young man did so.

"I ain't Emil Jackson. My name's Galde. Jack T. Galde."

"But—"

"Shut up!" Galde retrieved a Bowie knife from its sheath on his belt and walked up to the downed man.

"Whatcha doing now?"

"I'm gonna tie you up, boy, so you don't go hollering around that the bank's been robbed." He knelt behind him. The early morning light, shining in through the bank's front windows, glinted on the six-inch blade.

Galde rammed it down. Hard. Ormond convulsed as the steel sliced through his spine. The knife came down again and again, ripping up the man's back, shattering his nervous system.

Ormond's head lurched back. He twisted and flopped on the floor. Galde flipped him onto his back and drove the knive into the man's pulsating chest.

Stab. Hurt. Kill. Blood spread slowly over the polished marble floor.

Galde sheathed his knife in the living flesh again and again. The smell of blood rose up from the body as Bud Ormond kicked two last times and lay still.

Sweating, grinning, Galde rose, plunged the knife into the dead man's throat and stood back. Lugging his heavy saddlebags he slipped out the front door and walked around to the back of the bank.

Dawn broke fully in the east as he approached his horse. No one had seen him. He'd timed everything perfectly, down to the last detail. Galde chuckled and hefted the saddlebags onto his horse.

The yellow light illuminated dark red stains on his right hand and sleeve. Cursing, Galde threw down the bag, wiped off the blood with fresh oak leaves, ripped off his shirt and dressed in a fresh button-down.

Voices. One, high-pitched, was Betty Jane. He didn't know who the man was and didn't care. Betty Jane must be going into work early that day. He smiled, bent and lit the fuse with a sulphur match.

That done, Galde mounted his horse and rode up to Hawkin's Hotel.

Two men greeted him as he arrived there. The town was waking up, just in time to watch the show. He should have two more minutes. He walked inside, saw that the dining room wasn't open yet—as he knew it wouldn't be—and then walked out.

One minute.

A female scream pierced the dawn. Galde smiled. No more time. He looked at the bank.

The slow burning fuse met its end.

The explosion was intense, ear-shattering, as the five sticks of dynamite detonated. The building lurched on its foundations, rattled and slumped. Thousands of bricks noisily toppled as dust rose in a huge cloud. As it cleared, the Forestville Bank lay in ruins. Its ceiling had collapsed and all but one of the walls now lay scattered on the dirt.

"You there!" a male voice said. "Emil Jackson!"

Galde spun around. George Ryman, the barber, waved his shaving brush at him as he ran up. "What happened?"

"Hell if I know, Ryman. I was just trying to get some flapjacks when all of a sudden the whole place went up." He shook his head in mock anger and sorrow.

Ryman peered at the ruined bank. "Was anyone inside? Did anyone get killed?"

"I don't know. Didn't see anything."

Men and women ran out of hotels and their homes in every state of dress. The agitated people filled the street with their cries and shouts.

The barber shook his head. "Can't imagine something like this happening here." He cocked his head toward Galde. "Can you, Jackson?"

"Nope. Never came to mind."

Ryman threw up his hands and trailed off to join the crowd approaching the bank.

Galde joined them, mingled, expressed his shock and dismay, spoke of how he had fifty dollars in the safe. After twenty minutes of this—and well after the sheriff had found three bodies inside—he slipped away and mounted his horse.

Riding out of town, Galde finally allowed himself to smile. He guffawed, startling his mare, as he left Forestville behind him forever and rode out to find his next opportunity.

2

The passenger car rattled on its iron trail, jolting Spur McCoy from a drowse. He blinked twice, shook his head, sat up straight and pulled the telegram from his pocket.

His job didn't seem any easier upon re-reading the message. All that General Halleck had been able to give him were the bald facts: a string of small towns in Missouri and Kansas have been hit with bold bank robberies and murders. Five banks have been cleaned out. No witnesses attest to seeing anything of importance. Twelve men and three women—one pregnant—have been murdered in direct connection with the robberies.

Maybe that's why no witnesses are talking, he thought. They're dead. McCoy stuffed the telegram back into his pocket.

Staring at the length of ankle the fancily dressed woman seated across from him was daringly showing, he sighed. Not a hell of a lot to go on.

The thirtyish, red-haired woman smiled as she saw Spur eyeing her ankle. She smoothed down her skirt, cutting off his view, and straightened her back.

McCoy slumped in the seat and pushed his brown hat over his face. It was a long way to Kansas City, Missouri.

A far cry from most ex-soldiers, but Spur McCoy was now a member of the United States Secret Service, a branch of the federal government originally created by an act of Congress in the year 1865 to protect U.S. currency against counterfeiting, as well as to ensure its safety at all times.

Later, the Secret Service's duties were expanded to include those crimes which crossed state or territorial lines. Soon it became involved with other federal business, since it was the only federal agency with law enforcement personnel.

Fresh from a distinguished career in the Union Army, during which time he rose to the rank of captain, McCoy went to Washington, D.C. to serve as an aide to Senator Arthur B. Walton of New York, an old family friend.

He joined the Secret Service soon after it had been formed and served for six months in the Washington office. When his superiors realized that McCoy was not only a crack shot but the Service's best horseback rider, he was transferred to the St. Louis branch and was assigned to handle all cases west of the Mississippi River.

These two factors had been of the utmost importance in giving McCoy the dangerous assignments, for the law had only recently settled into most of the western United States and in some places hadn't quite done even that. Yet.

The work was tough. It commanded his absolute attention. Spur had no roots—no sweethearts, no established friends, no hometown affections. He was a loner. Though he'd had his share of pretty ladies his only constant companions were a Colt .45 at his hip, the Mexican coins ringing his hat, and a hankering to do justice.

Spur McCoy was the kind of man who was made for the untamed, turbulent American west: fearless and vigilant. He was making it into what he could.

The city withered under the burning summer sun. McCoy slapped his new mount's rump, strapped on his sparkling, serviceable saddle and walked the beast to the Kansas City General Mercantile. Broad Street was dusty and filled with countless horse droppings. After stocking up on coffee, beans, hard tack, canned peaches, pears and beef jerky, Spur loaded up the saddlebags, checked his carpetbag one last time, and headed for the local marshal's office.

Frank Porter was a big, ungainly man. His rough clothing hung on his frame and he extended a hand to McCoy.

Spur quickly explained his job. The marshal had heard of the robberies and spat into the dented spittoon when Spur mentioned them.

"Cowardly thieves!" he said. "They should thank their lucky stars they didn't hit my town. Hell, I'd have them all hanging by their necks if they'd come into Kansas City!"

Spur smiled. "That's why they didn't trouble you, Porter. Seems like these thieves avoid larger towns, preferring to do their dirty work in small, isolated ones. Less chance of being caught, more chance of being successful."

"Can't understand why there've been no witnesses," Porter said, chewing his lower lip. "It just don't seem right that nobody saw anything."

"Maybe those fresh bodies lying in the ground all over the state could tell us something," Spur grunted.

Porter glanced up at him. "Is that all you know?"

"So far."

"Not much to go on." The big man swatted a fly that buzzed around his sweating forehead.

"Nope. The robberies have all occurred on a fairly straight line heading west from here. I'm assuming they'll continue in that direction. Got a map?"

The man grunted, flipped open a creaky drawer in his desk and slapped a much-folded piece of paper onto it. "It's the best I have. Shows all the settlements and towns—and most of the large farms and ranches—from here to Colorado Territory. Some of it's even to scale."

Spur flopped into a chair and studied the map. Though crudely drawn it did indeed detail at least five more towns west of Jacksonville, the site of the last brutal, puzzling bank robbery.

"Can you get me a copy of this, Porter?" Spur asked.

The man smiled. "If you can wait a minute or so I can probably do one up."

The man soon covered a three-inch square piece of paper—the back of a whiskey bottle label he'd soaked off—with squiggly lines and uncertain block letters. Finished, he shoved the map over to Spur.

The Secret Service man nodded. "Guess that's the next place," McCoy said, stabbing his index finger on a tiny circle marked Holmes.

"Not much there," Porter said.

"Didn't think so. Is it big enough to make it worth a bank robber's time?"

The marshall mulled it over. "Sure, I guess. It's grown since I was out there last."

He folded up the map. "Thanks, Porter. Maybe I'll stop by on my way out once I've got this thing taken care of."

The lanky man grinned. "Ain't you cocksure. Why you so certain you can find those bastards? You don't know enough to piss at it."

Spur shrugged as he stuffed the map into his pocket. "It's my job."

Vanessa Thompson glanced out one of the paned windows that led from her parlor. A squat, dark figure walking down the street riveted her eyes. Vanessa gasped. Could it be? Yes, it was. It surely was. Her prayers had been answered. There, right there, walking down the street of Holmes, was a preacher man. Newly arrived, judging from the carpetbags he was carrying. A new preacher had come to Holmes!

She threw off her apron, gussied up her hair, and rushed out of her simple home.

"Excuse me, sir!" she called at the now departing figure. "Hello!"

Apparently oblivious to her, he kept up his steady, slow pace. Vanessa quickly overtook him and stopped before the man.

"Excuse me." She smiled broadly at the man who wore a simple dark suit and a clerical collar. "I was wondering if—if—"

"Yes?" The man's voice was soft, melodic. Above the white collar his face was fleshy, cleanly shaven, with small jowls, piercing black eyes and short-cropped hair.

Vanessa was pleased. "Well, it just has to be a sign from God that you've come to our town," she said quickly. "Here I've been praying for a new preacher for three weeks now and—and here you are!"

His smile broadened. "Are there souls to be saved here? Is there drinking? Fornicating? Dancing and gambling?"

Vanessa smirked. "You can't imagine—begging your pardon. Preacher, ever since my husband departed from this world of fleshly pleasures, leaving the church without a guiding light, the sin in this town has gone on unchecked." She shook her head. "I can barely buy a bolt of cloth or visit Aggie the milliner without running into one of those—well, *those* kind of women on the street!" Her cheeks paled. "I don't know who you are, why you're here or how long you can stay, but I'm ever so glad to see you!"

The preacher dropped his bags and spread out his arms. "With a welcome such as this, and with such a vivid portrait of this town's involvement with the Fiend, I believe the Lord has guided my footsteps." He looked into the sky above him. "This is where I was meant to go. This is my new home." He looked down at her. "If I can rely upon your help, dear sister of Christ, perhaps we can drive out the evil that thrives here."

Tears quelled up in Vanessa's eyes. "Yes. Yes! I—I—" She was speechless at this occurrence.

"Let us pray!"

And Jack T. Galde prayed.

The flat, featureless land had never known a mountain. One hour outside of Kansas City, endless acres of farmland stretched around Spur McCoy. Riding down the wide, dusty trail he passed fields of chin-high corn, green wheat and stubbly alfalfa. Spur hoped the towns Marshal Porter had mapped out were near the trail, as he'd indicated. Otherwise, they'd be swallowed up in the vast croplands.

Dozens of small farms and several fenced ranches dotted the area, as too did empty plots awaiting future human efforts. The land was dry, cracked and covered with scrawny weeds where streams and spring water hadn't yet been diverted to give it nourishing moisture.

Spur glanced his boots at his mount's flanks, urging her to pick up the speed. He was eager to begin his job.

Up ahead on the trail a figure lay sprawled on the ground. Spur rode quickly up to it. It was a woman. He halted his horse and rushed to her.

The blonde beauty lay face-up, one arm behind her back, eyes closed and fluttering. The rips in her red dress revealed much more than a woman should reveal in public. The woman's lips parted and locked together.

He didn't see powder burns or wounds. Spur touched her cheek. The woman opened her eyes and looked up at him. "Help me," she said in a pain racked voice.

Spur nodded. "Don't you worry, ma'am. I'll take care of you. What happened?"

This was puzzling. He didn't see anything physically wrong with her. Maybe she'd been raped . . .

"They came at me. I—I was walking to my sweetheart's ranch and they—they—" She squeezed her eyes shut and turned her head away from McCoy.

"I see."

"Water." She coughed. "I need water. And food."

He walked to his horse. As Spur reached for his canteen he heard rapid movement behind him.

"Hold it right there, mister!" a female voice said.

He turned, of course. The *injured* woman was on her feet, grinning and pointing the business end of a six-gun at his heart. She ran her left hand through her wild, dirty-blonde locks.

"Ma'am?" he asked.

"Don't you *ma'am* me, buzzard dick!" she spat. The blonde's eyes flashed at him. "I don't need your help. I don't need any man's help! I just need your money. Give it to me. Now! Empty your pockets!"

"Look, lady." Spur began. What the hell had he gotten himself involved in?

She racously laughed, maintaining her aim with a steady, sure hand. This was no injured woman. "Don't those big ears of yours work?" she asked in a gruff, unfeminine voice. "Cut the talk and hand over your money. Unless you wanna die out here in the dirt!"

Spur straightened his shoulders. This game had gone far enough. "You really don't wanna use that, woman! You think you can outshoot me?"

Jubilant chuckles emerged from her generous bosom. "You really want to find out?" She looked at him slyly. "Pa always said I was the best shot in the county. Heck, you don't know nothing about me. I've got the advantage. I caught you by surprise. You're just a dumb man." Her eyes were wild. "You and all men. You're pigs. Pigs! Buzzard dicks! And you're gonna throw your money down on the trail!"

"What're you gonna do after that?"

Spur relaxed. The woman was crazy, out of her mind. He'd talk her out of it.

She lifted her unplucked eyebrows. "Why, what I always do. I'll cut your balls off and make 'em into a purse!" The blonde hardened her visage. "Now give me your money?"

Spur smirked at her. "Just put down the gun and get on home, woman. I'd hate to have to kill you."

She hesitated, her cheeks flushing. The blonde's right hand trembled. "Oh—oh *hell!*" She threw down the gun.

Upon impact it discharged, sending a slug into the dirt and an explosion rippling through the hot summer air.

"Jesus!" Spur said. "You mean that thing was loaded?"

The woman looked at him. She arched her back, pressing her full breasts against the tattered bodice of her bright red dress. The material strained, threatened to unravel.

Spur allowed his gaze to travel below her chin. A pert, hard nipple peeked through the cloth.

"I didn't really wanna kill you," the woman said. She slid a hand between her legs. "I don't wanna kill any men. There's too much they can do for a lonely woman." She rubbed.

Spur shrugged and bent to retrieve her weapon. "Sorry, but I've got business to attend to."

Her right hand became more urgent, violently stroking her groin, pressing the thin material to her body. "Come on, mister! I *need* you! Right now!"

Spur was only human. The sight of the woman pleasuring herself in front of him, in broad daylight, set his body in motion. But he killed off the desire before it had a chance to build. "Sorry. I said no."

The blonde woman pouted. She gripped her bodice with her left hand and pulled hard. The material ripped apart and her dress fell to her ankles. Not a shred of cloth remained on her.

Wasn't she full surprises, Spur thought.

The harsh sunlight revealed every curve, every swell, every forbidden part of the woman's body. He stood, stunned, drinking her in. At least he could enjoy the show for a minute before he rode off to Holmes.

"Now, mister. Now!" the blonde said, her hand

moving up and down, pressing, rubbing, furrowing her yellow pubic hairs. Legs parted, knees bent, she rocked up and down as erotic sensations pulsed through her body. "I can't wait any longer. I can't! Git that thing out and use it on me! Come on!"

Her eyes locked onto his. She parted her lips, panting, writhing before him in unashamed ecstasy, giving him an open invitation to ravish her.

Spur felt himself responding again. He tried to fight it off but the woman's unexpected, outrageously sexual performance dug into his loins and wouldn't let go. She raised her left arm to him, her fingers parted, pleading.

Spur grunted as the pressure in his crotch rose to a painful, aching degree. He took a step toward her, mesmerized by the fire in her eyes, drinking in her passion, consumed by the lust she transmitted to him.

The blonde smiled as she rubbed herself. So near. So close. So willing. Spur walked to her. He dropped her now forgotten six-gun to the dirt, unbuckled his pants, ripped open the buttons and shoved them and his gunbelt to his feet.

"Yes! Now! Right now! I'm ready and wet!"

The words—their power—overwhelmed him. He stood before her in his long underwear. Her left arm closed around his waist, gripping him to her nude body.

No time for rational thought. No time for head-work. She was warm, soft. She crushed her full breasts against his shirt front. Spur looked down at the top of her yellow hair. No, he thought. No.

Yes!

"What the fuck're you doing with my wife?" a gruff voice barked behind him.

Spur threw the woman from him. He spun around, panting, to face the man who'd yelled at him.

3

"I said, what the hell're you doin' with my wife?"

The beefy, armed man glared at Spur, coughed and spat on the ground.

McCoy automatically reached for his Colt .45. Damn! It wasn't there!

"How the hell're you gonna grab your hogleg? You're standing in your underwear, asshole!"

"Your wife's plumb crazy," Spur said. He felt the tension in the air. "First she tried to kill me, then she offered herself up to me in such a way that no man could refuse."

The man smiled. "That's my Elsie." He glanced over McCoy's shoulder. "Come on over here, honey!"

The naked blonde strolled up to the gunman, stood beside him and smiled sweetly. "I done right?" she asked.

"Yeah, honey, you done right. Just like I told you

to do. Sure got him all fired up, thinking you'd let him stick it in. You did a good job, Elsie; didn't leave nothin' out."

"What the hell's goin' on here?" Spur asked.

The big man snarled. "Don't go usin' filthy language like that in front of my Elsie!" he thundered. "I've killed a man for less than that!"

"You're as crazy as she is," Spur said.

It had been a trap, of course. A well-planned, well-executed trap. They'd gotten him right where they wanted him.

The thick man grunted. "Hell no! Neither of us are. Just a little trick I dreamed up one night while I was packing it to her." He fingered her hair with his left hand. "Back to business. Kick yer pants off yer boots and walk backwards. And no tricks! Try anything and your guts'll be sizzling in the sunshine!"

Spur sighed. This wasn't his day. "What kind of a man are you? You'd use your pretty wife to rob innocent men?"

He snorted. "Hell, I'd have my mama spread 'em to get a few extra dollars—if I didn't think she'd scare 'em away. Now do it! Don't bend over, just kick 'em off."

Spur worked his pants lower, twisting his legs, pulling, tugging at them, alternating boots. He finally freed all but the waistband. He looked down. From the man's viewpoint they should look like they were still tangled up.

"That's as much as I can do. They must've caught on the heels."

The gunman snarled. "You think I'm that stupid? Try harder, asshole!"

"Check them yourself."

"Elsie, go over there and do what you do best—get that man's pants off!"

The bare assed young woman smiled, walked to McCoy and bent over.

Spur slipped his left boot up into the air. He caught his gunbelt as it sailed up in front of him. McCoy simultaneously pulled the blonde to him and unholstered his Colt. A second later he had its muzzle pressed against the screaming woman's throat.

"Sonofabitch!" the big man said as he dropped his aim. His eyes grew wide. "You move faster than a rattler!"

"You're gonna lose Elsie faster than that if you don't drop your weapon and ride outa here!" Spur warned him.

He laughed. "Hell, kill her. I can always get another cunt. Plenty more like that out there!"

"You bastard!" the woman screamed.

"I don't believe you," McCoy said. "She's too valuable to you. What other woman would live with an ugly, fat coward like you? A man who has to hide behind a woman to separate innocent men from their money?"

The man blubbered. "*Coward?*—you—I'll—"

"I'm calling your bluff! You won't do nothing except what I tell you to do. Understood?"

The big man's face reddened as he nodded. "Damn! I had it all planned. Everything. Elsie and me practiced for two weeks. This was our first time!"

"Ah, you're making my heart bleed for you! Now throw that gun onto the dirt and get your fat butt outa my sight!''

"What—what about Elsie?''

Spur paused. "Hell, I'll worry about that when I don't have to see your ugly face! She's a looker.''

"Now wait a minute—''

"Drop it!''

He sighed, cursed, snorted and threw the gun into the dust.

"Move!'' Spur commanded.

The big man turned and walked down the trail toward Kansas City, kicking the dirt, hollering and moaning.

When he was out of sight Spur released the woman. Elsie turned to him, trembling, her eyes bright with fear.

"Are you gonna—I mean—''

Spur smiled as he retrieved his pants and dressed. "No. Just don't try that again, little lady. Is he really your husband?''

She nodded. "He forced me into it. I don't mind saying I enjoyed teasing you—you're a handsome man. But I hate him!'' The bitterness in her voice was convincing.

"Best thing I can think of for you to do is to leave your husband as fast as you can and settle down somewhere else. Get him out of your life.''

She nodded. "I suppose you're right.''

McCoy gathered up the two weapons, stuffed them into his saddlebags and mounted. Before he rode off he looked back at the fetching, naked woman. "And get some clothes on, you hear?''

"Yeah, might as well.''

Spur rode off for Holmes.

* * *

Joshua Golden, Jack T. Galde thought as he scrubbed his face in his hotel room. That was his name. A new name, a new profession, a new town ripe for the picking. He'd installed himself in a matter of hours.

With the support of Vanessa Thompson, the concerned, church-going citizens had flocked to him. The late hours he'd spent boning up on the Bible, recalling the lessons his mother had given him on her knee when he was a screaming brat, had paid off. He'd fooled them all with his talk of God and Satan and Heaven.

Hal Phillips, Holmes' unoffical lawman, attended church every Sunday morning. So did the mayor, half the citizenry and the largest depositor in the Western Bank. He'd worked his way into the puny power circles of the town, gained the people's confidence, worked hard to establish a reputation as an honest man of God.

It had been difficult—excruciatingly difficult. He'd had to lay off liquor and never got to watch the dancing girls at the Glittering Garter Saloon. He hadn't had a woman for over a month. Late at night that tore him up inside. But he knew that in the long run it was well worth it. He'd live a life of luxury as soon as he'd stripped this town of its wealth.

Galde wiped the chilling water from his face. He'd done it. He'd made his moves and carefully planned. Now he'd wait until the time was right.

Holmes, Kansas, was a small town west of Kansas City. Named after its colorful founder, Quentin Holmes, it was a gathering place for local farmers and ranchers to buy, sell, exchange goods and to do some drinking.

Quentin Holmes, now deseased, was a man who appreciated the finer things in life—especially *art*. At least, that's what he told the first residents. After building the bank, church and general store, he'd established the lavish Glittering Garter Saloon. Every night, 'ladies', imported from various shady parts of various shady eastern cities, put on a show that made the local men drink more and think less.

Though the founder had died years ago, the saloon was still the center of the life for most of the men who lived there.

Spur rode into the town that had been carved out of a centuries old, dried river bed. He checked into a hotel, discarded his carpetbag, rubbed cold water on his face and set about to business.

He stood on the boardwalk that fronted the Calvin Hotel, hands on his hips, thinking, looking around.

"Excuse me, but you look lost," a pleasantly feminine voice said behind him.

McCoy was pleased at the voice's owner. A well-formed, primly-dressed woman in her late thirties smiled at him in a wholesome manner. Twirling a white parasol over her left shoulder, she chuckled, "You look *very* lost. Can I be of any help?"

Spur tipped his hat. "Thanks, ma'am; just got into town." He was somewhat irritated by the interruption but figured she might be some value to him.

"Well, there's not much here—not really." The

woman proffered her right hand. "I'm Vanessa Thompson, widow of Charles Thompson."

Spur took it gently. "Spur McCoy."

Withdrawing her hand, she lowered her parasol. "It is powerfully hot out here today. Would you like to come to my parlor? I'm afraid I've never been much of a woman who could stand heat."

"Gladly, Mrs. Thompson."

They'd soon installed themselves in the widow's front room in the small, plain house beside the church.

"Well, what's your business here in Holmes, if you don't mind my asking?"

"Not at all." He took the cup of cool tea that she offered him and began spinning a cover story. "I've just left St. Louis looking for a place to settle down. I'm a printer and was thinking to start a newspaper."

"A *newspaper?* In Holmes?" She laughed. "Mr. McCoy, I assume you've already decided that this isn't the place. Why, most of the folks around here don't read. I know that because they haven't read the Bible, the only book *worth* reading. And furthermore, nothing ever happens worth reporting! It's a lazy town with lazy people."

"That may be," Spur said, and sipped the cool liquid, "but I've heard Holmes is growing. How many people live here now?"

"Oh, let's see—I'd say about two hundred or so— but mind you, most of them have farms and ranches nearby. Maybe about fifty in Holmes itself."

Spur nodded. "Many new folks moving in here?"

Vanessa shook her head. "Not many. Let's see—
there's been three in the last month. That's quite a
few. A young girl by name oh—oh, I can't remember, flounced into town yesterday in a scarlet dress
with even brighter lips." She sniffed. "The young
lady—if I can dare to call her that—is working in
the Glittering Garter Saloon." She smiled broadly.
"And two weeks ago the Reverend Joshua Golden
answered my prayers. He's been preaching every
Sunday. A fine enough man, though perhaps his
style's a little soft for my sake. Reverend Golden's
doesn't drum up nearly the thunder that my late
husband used to call down in the pulpit." She
allowed herself a fond memory—it flickered across
her face like a summer breeze. "And then some
drifter showed up here a few days ago." She curled
up her nose. "Someone should inform him of the
values of regular bathing."

"And that's a lot?" Spur shook his head. "Guess
this might not be the place for a newspaper. Still,
I'll be around for a few days, thinking about where
to check next." He placed his cup on the small
table beside his chair and rose. "Thanks for your
hospitality, ma'am."

She nodded pleasantly at him. "I hope to see you
in church Sunday morning if you're still in town.
Preacher Golden told me he's planning a soul-
searching sermon and I don't think you should
miss it!"

"No promises, Mrs. Thompson, but I'll do my
best." He walked to the door.

"And if you see that brazen hussy on the street,
tell her I'm expecting here there, too!"

Spur walked out into the relentless sunlight. The

drifter Vanessa had mentioned was a possibility—
not a strong one, but a possibility. Of course, a gang
could ride into town at any moment and rob the
bank.

But that didn't fit the picture. These thieves did
things quietly. They were smart.

He began to wonder if Holmes was the thieves'
next target. It seemed too small, even for a western
town, even with the riches of the surrounding
farmers and ranchers that had presumably been
deposited in the small bank that he was passing.

Still, it was something to go on.

Reaching the front of the Sullivan Hotel, Spur
stared at his new mount as it quietly lapped at the
trough. The drifter might be one of the thieves, but
it wasn't likely. He'd check him out just in case.
And after that?

He stroked the horse's smooth, shimmering
flank. Maybe he should leave Holmes, move on to
the next town. Even now the thieves might be
killing more innocent people. Even as he stood
here another safe might be suffering from the blast
of dynamite. Even then—

"Becky!" a dusty man in riding clothes yelled as
he bustled up to Spur.

"Sorry to disappoint you but I'm not your
Becky." Spur's voice was sarcastic as the hulking
man stormed up to him across the dusty street.
"She sure must be an ugly gal for you to mistake
me for her!"

"Not you, asshole!" the man said. "The horse!"
He curled is upper lip before looking down. His
sunburned face blossomed into a boyish grin,
exuding joy as he gazed at Spur's new horse.

"Becky, where ya been? Huh? I never thought I'd see you again, you old girl!" He reached out for the mare's neck.

Spur blocked his hand. "Begging your pardon, sir, but that's my horse you're ogling. Kindly keep your hands off."

The narrow-eyed rancher grabbed McCoy's arm and wrestled it away. "The hell I will! I'll touch my own horse whenever I want! This here's my Becky. I'd know her in a minute!"

"You're wrong," Spur said.

"Bullshit!" His face reddened. "Someone stole her off my ranch three days ago. I've been up day and night since then lookin' for her." He drew his gun, his face showing the strain of unaccustomed thought. "You must've stole her! You must've been the one! Now give her back right now!"

"Come on, mister! You made a mistake!"

"No. You're the one who's made the mistake, horse thief!"

He cocked his revolver.

4

"Try to stop me!" the big man yelled. "I don't mind shooting a horse thief! Hell, that's legal around these parts. That's my Becky. You stole her from me and boy, we don't cotton to your kind around here!"

Spur waved off the armed man. "Hey, look, I don't know what you've been drinking, mister, but that's my horse. I bought her fair and square in Kansas City just this morning. Paid fifty genuine U.S. dollars for her. So if I were you, mister, I'd holster my weapon and try to think things out before you go and accuse me of being a horse thief!"

The rancher spat. "Hah! I know my Becky when I see her! Can't imagine why you'd be so stupid to bring her here right after you stole her, but I figure that's what you is—stupid!" He waved his six-gun

37

menacingly. "You just back off, boy, and let me take Becky home with me!"

Spur controlled his anger. "This isn't your horse. I bought her. She's mine."

The man guffawed. "An' I suppose you got a bill of sale, right?"

"Damn straight I do!" Spur pushed his right hand into his pocket and retrieved the small paper. He thrust it out toward the man. "All legal and everything. I don't think your horse thief stole her, rode her out to Kansas City and sold her all in the space of three days!" he said as the big man peered at the paper.

"It's possible." He squinted, staring at the receipt as if it were written in Chinese.

"Try to think straight, pal. This isn't your Becky. This isn't your horse. She's mine." Spur grabbed her reins protectively. "It's all there. Read it!"

The rancher's shoulder slumped as he stared at the bill of sale. "Hell, I—I don't know. Never was much for letters." He glanced up. "Hey Hal, git your butt over here and read this here thing for me!" He waved it in the air.

A thin man with thick glasses sauntered up. "What seems to be the trouble, Burt?" he asked.

"Just read it!"

"Okay, okay."

"This man seems to think I stole his horse," Spur threw in. "I can't convince him otherwise."

"Well, you've convinced me," the man said, after scanning the paper. "This horse is your rightful property. If you did steal his Becky, this isn't her. Sorry, Burt; it's all here. This horse was purchased this morning in Kansas City."

Burt stomped on the ground. "Damn. Hell! I was sure this was my Becky!" He looked wildly at the thin man. "How we know he didn't just get someone to write that up all fancy like? Couldn't he've done that?"

"It looks good to me. Besides, he wouldn't bring her here to town."

Spur patted the mare's head. "Anyone can make a mistake, Burt." He snatched the bill of sale from Hal's hand. "Hope you find your horse—wherever she is."

"Sorry for the trouble, stranger. I'm Hal Phillips, the unofficial law in these parts. Well come on, Burt; let's have a drink. Think you need a cooling down."

"Well. . . . well . . ." he stammered. "I still think that's my Becky!"

Spur shook his head as the two men walked off. He patted his horse once again and rambled down the street, taking in what few sights the small town had to offer. He tipped his hat at two elderly women who, upon seeing him, nodded politely but scurried away. He saw a young man walking hand in hand with a freckle-faced girl, the two of them oblivious to anything but each other.

A block down the street a pudgy, sweating, hatless man dressed in black—with a backwards white collar—approached him. As soon as he saw Spur the man hurried forward.

"Hello. New in town?" the man asked, mopping his slick forehead with a stained handkerchief.

"Sure am. Just arrived today."

"Well, on the behalf of Holmes, let me welcome you to our town. My name's Golden. Joshua

Golden." He grabbed his jacket lapels.

"You must be the new preacher Vanessa Thompson told me about."

"You've met Mrs. Thompson? Fine woman, she is. A fine sister of Christ." He shook his head. "Well, I've got some sick folk to attend to. Hope to see you in church on Sunday. I've got a powerful sermon cookin' in my brain!"

"Don't know if I'll be around that long, but if so I'll try to make it," Spur said, somewhat half-heartedly.

Reverend Golden didn't seem to notice. "You do that. Good afternoon!"

With that the man was gone, hurrying down the street.

Spur returned to his hotel room, cleaned his Colt .45 and took a short nap. He didn't know why he was staying in Holmes. The place seemed quiet enough, and the only reason he'd gone there was the assumption that the thieves would rob the local bank. He had no evidence to support this except a stubborn idea in the back of his head.

McCoy flopped down on the hard, small bed and thought it all out.

Later, after dark, Spur once again roamed the streets of Holmes. By the light of the nearly full moon he saw a dirty man, dressed in tattered clothing, walking aimlessly, dragging his left foot.

The drifter?

Spur sank back into a heavy shadow and watched the man for a few minutes. He looked into windows, stood outside a hotel for a while and stared inside before wandering off.

McCoy sighed. He didn't seem the kind of man who'd murder innocent people and rob banks. If he had he certainly wouldn't be so poor, and Spur guessed that the man wasn't in some sort of disguise. Anyone who went to those lengths to rob a bank would probably enjoy the fruits of his dirty work.

The drifter seemed harmless. Spur shrugged and headed into the nearest bar. He might as well have a drink.

Jack T. Galde pulled at the hot, constricting collar around his neck as he strolled. He hated the damn thing, hated the town he was in, hated pretending to be a preacher. Most of all he hated that fuckin' Vanessa Thompson, the widow lady who watched his every move as if she was testing him. Hell, he'd like to throw down a bottle of whiskey and show her how much a man of the cloth he really was.

Of course, he couldn't do that. Too much was riding on this. Through discreet inquiries he'd discovered that the local bank had deposits in excess of $20,000—a huge sum, compared to what he's been getting lately. Some of it was held in trust for one of the founding father's nephews who lived on an outlying ranch with his adopted parents.

For that much money he could force himself to wait a few more weeks until he got back to enjoying the finer things of life.

Speaking of, Galde thought, as he spied a blond-haired, beautiful girl waltzing down the boardwalk toward him. She was a magnificent creature, all hair and lips and breasts and thighs, wrapped up in a tight green dress.

She was the kind of woman that any man would want. The kind of woman he wanted right then. Damn! What in hell gave him the idea to dress up in that old preacher's outfit he'd stolen a while back? Why couldn't he just be an ordinary man here? If he was he'd take that delicious package, rip off her clothing and pound it into her until she screamed for mercy.

He felt lust seize his veins. He didn't stop looking at the girl as she approached him. Seeing his outfit, the young woman slowed her steps.

Galde's face twisted up into hatred—not at the girl, but at the way he'd tricked himself into denying the good things of life. "Young woman, are you a Christian girl?"

She looked down as she walked up to him. "That's not for me to say, reverend."

Inwardly, he hoped not. Maybe he'd have time for one quick—no. Not now. "Find out. Come to church this Sunday. It'll do you good."

Hell, it'd do *him* good, seeing her there while he sweated his way through another one of those damn, demanding, exhausting sermons. He could glance at her tits every time he said the word "God."

"Sorry, preacher; I always sleep late on Sundays." With a dazzling, white-toothed smile, she skipped away and disappeared into the Glittering Garter Saloon.

Damn her! Galde pulled at the collar again and trudged off to visit the sick old woman who'd just willed her entire fortune to the church. At least he could pick up a hundred or so before he hit the bank—if the old broad managed to kick off soon. Very soon.

He sighed. The problems of being a preacher in a Kansas city town. Galde didn't know if it was worth it.

The man turned around and looked back at the Glittering Garter Saloon. Maybe he could meet one of the girls who worked there, somehow, someway, pay her enough money to keep her mouth shut and have a little fun with her.

Sure. He could hire a carriage for her and they could meet out of town some afternoon. He'd tell her to bring a bottle of whiskey and pay her fifty bucks for the little adventure.

He felt excitement course through him as he planned it out. That could take care of his worst cravings for a week or so until he was figuring on leaving anyway.

Then he sighed. It was too risky. He couldn't do anything that might ruin the image he'd built up for himself in Holmes. Not with that damned Vanessa Thompson breathing down his neck every second.

If she found out about it—and she had her ways and spies—he'd be kicked out by the townsfolk. Once he'd lost their trust he'd have to move on to the next town.

No. He'd worked too hard, suffered through too much bullshit to ruin it now.

He'd just have to play the upstanding, clean-living preacherman for a week more. Just a week.

Well, maybe less. Five days. He thought of the blonde girl.

Four.

Spur stood at the bar, nursing a whiskey, staring at the assorted townfolk there. The stage was bare, empty, but a large sign next to it promised the wonders of real female flesh every night. *Dancing girls,* it said. Chorines with class!

He snorted, thinking he'd have to come back there later. Hell, he didn't mind a good show.

McCoy nearly dropped his glass as he saw Vanessa Thompson, dressed in a demure black dress and matching bonnet, storm into the place.

He rushed over to greet her at the door. "Mrs. Thompson. What brings you to this place?"

She eyed the glass in his hand and shook her head. "What do you think? I'm here to warn these men of the dangers of alcoholic beverages," Vanessa said smugly. "I can see you need my words as well. I also have to warn the good men of this town of the threat of loose women; to try to open these men's eyes to the lascivious, licentious behavior that goes on in this kind of establishment!"

"Now hold on, Mrs. Thompson," Spur said. "I'm pretty sure they're aware of these facts. And just as sure that they'd heard all this from you before. Am I right?"

"Well—well—that doesn't matter!" Her voice was filled with righteous wrath. "It's my duty to carry on the work of my late Charles—God rest his soul—in cleaning up this town of the evils of drink and filthy women!"

"What about the Reverend Golden?" Spur asked kindly. "Isn't that his job?"

The woman harrumphed. "I'm not so sure about the man. He preaches well enough, but he doesn't seem real. He doesn't smoke. He doesn't drink. He doesn't go with the ladies."

Spur tucked his chin against his chest. "Isn't that the way a preacher's supposed to act?"

"Yes, but they don't. Not out here, anyway. And it's just not right for a man of the cloth not to be a man of women, too. What I mean is, he should be married. Men like him make me suspicious of all kinds of things." She arched her left eyebrow.

"Mrs. Thompson, I don't want to dissuade you of your noble goal, but do you really think you'll accompolish anything in here?"

"If you try to stop me I'll be certain that you're a true instrument of the Devil rather than just a sinner," she warned him.

Spur set down his drink and tipped his hat to her. "In that case, I'll be leaving now. Good evening, Mrs. Thompson."

She ignored him.

"Hey Vanessa!" a man called out as Spur was headed out the batwing doors. "You gonna put on a show fer us?"

"Yeah. Show us your ankles! Hoo-whee!"

"Jesus will forgive you for your sins!" she hollered, "if you confess your—"

Spur left, shaking his head. As he emerged from the saloon, the drifter passed by him and headed down the block. Curious, Spur followed.

The man seemed to be going toward a specific location. Within moments he'd halted before the darkened general store. The drifter didn't look around. He simply tried the door knob.

After struggling with it for a few moments, he cursed lightly and kicked in the front window, sending it to the floor inside in a tinkling crash.

Spur ran toward him. "Hey! What the hell do you think you're doing?"

The drifter pushed out splinters of glass and jumped inside.

5

Spur bolted to the general store. Reaching it, he peered through the shattered window. All was dark inside, and the drifter wasn't in sight.

He carefully stepped through the yawning frame and drew his .45. Broken glass crunched beneath his boots. The drifter might not be a bank-robber, but he was certainly a thief.

"Where are you?" he called into the darkness. "Show yourself, drifter!"

Nothing. Spur surveyed the large store. It was packed to the ceiling with every conceivable kind of dry good. One whole wall was filled with dozens of bolts of cloth. Nearby were hand tools, wire, nail kegs, rope, whips, bags that probably held seed and lime. To the rear of the store were cracker barrels, stacks of dusty canned goods, shadowy mirrors and dozens of other items.

"I said, show yourself!" he hollered again.

A glint. A whine. A glistening blade shot through the air a foot from McCoy's head and plunged into the door behind him.

"Son of a bitch!" Spur said.

Another knife flashed by him.

Spur ducked behind a solid oak counter covered with cast-iron pots and cauldrons. A clang told him of a third knife's passage.

"What the hell do you want?" Spur asked.

"Food. I'm hungry. Starvin'! And the people around here don't give a shit about that, about me. So I figured I'd just rustle up my own vittles."

"By breaking into this store? Not smart, drifter."

The voice was issuing from the far corner. Spur glanced above the counter. Straining his eyes through the murky store he made out a large wooden plaque filled with countless knifes of every size and kind nailed to the far wall.

A hand reached up and snatched one.

McCoy ducked. "Put the knife down, drifter! Give yourself up. At least they'll feed you in jail."

"Never!" he shouted. "I ain't going back there! That's what got me in this mess in the first place!"

So words wouldn't help, Spur thought, as the sound of steel against iron rang through the darkened store again. He darted across the open floor to the end of the long counter that stretched across the back. Crouching behind it, Spur waited. He knew the drifter was at its far end, below the knife display.

"Leave me alone! All I want's something to eat!"

Spur moved past the counter and pressed up against the rear wall. There he was—a down-cast, shrunken-shouldered man leaning against the corner. Spur saw a line of canvas bags on a shelf above his head. Might come in handy, he thought.

"I'll get you!" the man grabbed another knife and tossed it at the pots and pans again, then saw Spur.

"No!" he said, reaching up. His hand met empty wood.

Spur easily peeled off a shot six feet above the drifter's head. The bullet pierced a sack. A stream of white flour poured down directly on the drifter.

He coughed, gagged, wiping at his eyes as the bag unloaded its contents.

McCoy laughed as he strode over to the man. He grabbed one of his flailing arms and hauled him to his feet. Yanking him out of the flour shower, Spur shook his head. "I think you need to visit—what's his name? Hal Phillips?"

With that he pulled the man out of the store, through the opened window, down the street and into the saloon. McCoy was pleased to see Vanessa Thompson had left.

"Where's Hal Phillips live?" he yelled. "Got a ghost for him."

The lanky man with bottle-thick glasses emerged from the smoky air. "I'm Phillips. What the hell's going on now?" he asked.

"Here." Spur thrust the flour-covered man at him. "Caught the drifter trying to rob the general store. He broke a window and scattered some knives around."

"Olsen Hunter?" Hal seemed a bit dazed by the news, but fairly pleased by Spur's accomplishment. "Well, thanks—I think," he said, surveying the coughing man. "Guess I'll lock him up in my house. What'd you say your name was?" the unofficial lawman asked.

Spur shrugged and walked to the bar. "Didn't."

Phillips shrugged. "Well, come on, Hunter." He dragged the sneezing man from the saloon.

Spur ordered a whiskey, got it and tried to pay the hefty barkeep.

"Nothin' doing," the apron said, smiling. "We need more law-abiding citizens like you around here. This one's on the house. Why not get a table and enjoy the show? It's just about to start."

Grinning, Spur thanked the man and sat at the back of the saloon. Within minutes every table was filled as the men of the surrounding area poured in for their nightly visual orgy.

A mustached, white-suited man slammed his hands down on the keyboard of a small piano next to the stage. "Gentlemen! Prepare your eyes for the vision of the one, the only, Glitter Garter Revue!"

The 30 men hollered, stomped their feet and otherwise greeted the news with enthusiasm. The piano player started in on some nameless tune. Four young women—attired in petticoat-stuffed dresses with plunging necklines—spilled out from a small door and onto the tiny stage.

They launched into a dance number. What it lacked in artistic merit, Spur thought, was compensated for by the amount of female flesh it exposed. The four girls shook, romped, highkicked and bounced around, showing as much or more than their counterparts anywhere in the country.

One young lass particularly intrigued Spur. Mounds of blonde hair lay piled on her head. She wore a dress of the brightest scarlet silk and her face shone as she moved through the routine, struggling with the simple dance steps. When the other three girls kicked, she bounced; when they bounced, she kicked.

Spur sat back in his chair and enjoyed the sight of the increasingly exasperated blonde. He didn't mind if she didn't know what she was doing, and from the whoops around him he was certain no one else did either.

The girls performed four songs, bowed low to show off their ample cleavage and, giggling, disappeared in the little room next to the stage.

The piano player quickly positioned himself in front of the door. "The girls will be out shortly, men, so try to hold yourselves back."

Spur smiled. He wanted to talk with the blonde. He wanted to buy her a drink. McCoy walked to the bar, borrowed a pencil from the apron, wrote a short note and handed it to the piano player with a silver dollar.

"Would you give this to the blonde?" he asked.

He studied it. "Sure. But you might have to wait your turn. Patrice is new here. None of the men know her." He smirked and pocketed the note.

Soon after, the girls emerged. Spur sat upright as the piano player handed the blonde his note. She looked over to where he pointed, beamed and walked to his table as McCoy rose.

"Glad you decided to accept my invitation. Can I buy you a drink, Miss. . . ."

"Carlon. Patrice Carlon. And I'd love one! A

sarsaparilla is fine."

Spur quickly got her one and returned to his table.

"I was so surprised when Jack pointed you out to me. I never had a man write me a note." The girl had a dazzling smile, perfect white teeth, a short nose and wide-open, staring blue eyes.

"I heard you were new here."

"I'm new anywhere. This is my first night. Well," she said, making a face. "My first night of *this* kind of dancing. I guess I'm not very good at it."

"I thought you were fine. A little rusty, but fine. And the men sure did like you."

She blushed. "I'm not used to all this attention— or all these men." She shivered. "Look, mister—"

"My name's McCoy. Spur McCoy."

She nodded. "Mr. McCoy, I'm not comfortable here. I hate to think what else these men want me to do for them. Or with them. Would you mind walking me back to my hotel?" Patrice fluttered her eyelashes.

He stood. "It would be an honor, Miss Carlon."

She giggled. "My, aren't you one with the fancy manners!"

Patrice took his arm and they strolled to her hotel.

Once at her door, she turned to him. "Won't you come inside?"

Spur accepted at once. She turned up the lamps as Spur locked the door.

"I hope you don't think I'm too forward," Patrice said, standing nervously in the center of her room.

He leaned against the door. "I don't think you're too *anything*, Miss Carlon."

She laughed nervously. "It's just that I figure, well, I mean, if I'm supposed to dance for all those men, and—and—, well you know, I figure I better know how." She looked up at him and squished her cheeks to her nose. "Know what I mean?"

"You've never been with a man?"

She threw her head back and laughed throatily. "Oh, heck, I've been with them. Not as many as the other girls. Just a few when I could get away from my parents." Patrice stared into his eyes. "But St. Louis doesn't grow many like you, Mr. McCoy. I think you could teach me a thing or two." Despite her bold words the young woman's cheeks colored.

"Call me Spur." He walked to her and touched her arm. "You sure about this?"

"Sure I'm sure." She pulled his arm to her waist and touched his chest. "Take off your hat, mister."

He flung it to the ground.

"Now your shirt. Take that off too!" Her voice was breathy.

Grinning, Spur unbuttoned it and let it fall to the ground. "You sure you haven't done this much, Miss Carlon? You sound pretty experienced to me."

"Not experienced," she said. "Just desperate. Kick off your boots and take off your pants." She sat on the bed, leaned back against the pillows and watched him. "I just gave you a show; now give me one!"

The boots were off in seconds. Spur unbuckled his belt and dropped his dusty trousers. He stood in his long underwear.

Patrice raised her eyebrows. "My, my, Spur, what a large bulge you have there. Could I be the cause of that pulsing growth?"

He grinned. "You know damn well you are, woman! Come on over here and take these off for me!"

"No. I wanna see you stripped naked. All the men I've been with always doused the lights before they did me. Or we were outside at night. I wanna see what a real man looks like!" She leaned back, waiting.

Grunting, Spur bent and ripped off the cotton underwear. He stood up, fully erect and gazed down at the blonde woman. "Well?" he asked. "You're seeing me now. You're seeing what you're doing to me with that pretty little mouth of yours!"

She giggled, gazing at his crotch. "I'm seeing you. I'm seeing more of you than I ever thought any man had!" She gulped. "Now show me what you can do with that thing! Rip my dress off and ride me, Spur!"

He jumped onto the bed beside Patrice and rolled her on top of him. McCoy fumbled with the buttons that ran down the back of Patrice's dress, cursed and ripped it, splaying the red material. He rustled it off the laughing woman and tore her petticoats into shreds, flinging them all over the bed as he lustily denuded her.

Patrice Carlon was on fire. She ground her crotch to his and kissed his chin and cheeks.

"You taste good," she said, running her tongue along the line of his stubbly jaw.

McCoy grunted and turned her onto her back. He

forced her legs apart and knelt between them. "Don't be so shy, Patrice," he said.

"I will if you will," she teased.

"Okay." He bent his head and took the woman's left nipple into his mouth. It hardened under his tongue, stiffened as he sucked her firm breast.

She groaned, gripped his head and forced his mouth lower, pushing deeper until he'd taken half her breast.

"Oh. Ohhh!"

Spur relished the sweet, warm flesh, the way her nipple responded, the groans that escaped from her lips. He lifted his head and enmouthed its twin, sucking, gnawing on its hard tip as she shook his head.

He rose and proudly stroked his erection, staring down at the overheated woman.

"You want this?" he asked, smirking.

She stared down at his huge organ. "Yes. Of course I do! Haven't I made myself clear?" She spread her legs and raised her crotch to him. "Put it in me. Go ahead, Spur. Stick it into my pussy."

"I don't know. I thought I'd suck on your tits for an hour or so first to really get you worked up. Thought we could take our time."

"I *am* worked up!" she said, impatient.

Spur moved his body down to hers. Gripping his hard penis, he pushed it against her wet opening and shoved. Patrice arched her back as he slid into her, filling her, stretching her like she'd never been stretched before, slowly driving her out of her mind.

"Oh, Oh god, Spur!" the woman wailed.

Their pubic hairs entwined as he sank full-length

into her. Spur gripped her head and slammed his
lips onto hers. He pushed his tongue against
Patrice's lips and into her liquid mouth, darting it
toward her throat.

She moaned as their mouths thrashed together.
The urgency at McCoy's loins drove him to
withdraw and push back in, slowly, lovingly. The
young woman dug her fingers into his muscled
back as he began riding her, pumping, pounding
between her parted legs.

Spur lifted his mouth. "This is what you
wanted," he said, ramming into her. "You wanted
to be fucked hard and fast. You wanted my cock in
your tight little pussy."

"Yes. Yes!" Her eyes were half-closed as she
writhed beneath him, lifting her hips to meet his
with every powerful thrust. Patrice tossed her
head, flinging blonde hair all over the pillow as he
rammed into her.

Spur's scrotum banged repeatedly against her
buttocks as he drove his penis deeper, deeper.
They locked together, their slick bodies molding
into one as Patrice gripped him with animalistic
passion.

"God. Jesus! You're so tight and hot!" he
moaned as he filled and emptied her vagina.

Patrice stared at him. "Give it to me. Slam it in!
Set my pussy on fire!" Her eyes were alive with
erotic heat as they burned into his. "Deeper.
Harder! Come on, Spur; fuck me!"

He pumped faster, his hips blurring as he
slammed into her velvety orifice. The familiar yet
ever-new sensations made his testicles boil and

heated him until droplets of hot sweat rained down onto the woman's body.

Below him, Patrice closed her eyes. Harsh, short breaths blasted out between her slick lips. She screwed up her face and strangled out a cry as he sent her over the edge, into the dark, shuddering place that sent bolts of electricity ripping through her, reducing her to a trembling, spasming woman that clutched him in her ecstasy.

Her climax was too much for Spur to take. She tightened around him, wringing his stiff penis. He felt his control fade as their bodies slammed together.

"Fill me up!" the gasping woman said, her face bright red. "Give it to me! Shoot your ball-juice!"

That did it. Waves of intense, bone-jarring excitement coursed through him. Grunting, jerking his hips spastically, he ejaculated deep into her, squirting, spewing hot male seed as he plowed.

Pleasure thundered through him. The room tilted, swerved before his lust-blinded eyes as he emptied himself with each savage thrust. His climax went on and on, extended to an incredible length as Patrice slapped her arms around his sticky torso and pushed her breasts against him.

After an unmeasurable time Spur felt drained. He gasped, puffing his breath against her hair. They relaxed. Muscles loosened. Their bodies slapped down onto the dripping bed, their hearts racing in time with each other as Patrice continued to grip his penis in orgasm-induced contractions.

They lay there, joined, panting, for five minutes. Spur finally lifted his head and looked down at her.

Patrice Carlon's face glowed. Her eyes twinkling, she stuck out her tongue and pantomimed extreme exhaustion, sucking in her breath in a comic style.

Spur laughed. "Hell, Patrice, I gotta remember to stay away from you."

She squeezed harder around his softening penis. "What makes you say that?"

"You could be hazardous to my health." He kissed the top of her head. "I don't think you need any more practice, Patrice. You sure know how to get a guy all hot and bothered."

Patrice smiled. "You complaining? You didn't seem to mind a few minutes ago. You got so wild, so furious, that I didn't know what you'd do."

Spur cupped her left breast. "No, I'm not complaining. Hell no! You drove me out of my mind, woman. Besides, you knew exactly what I'd do." He smirked and started to pull away from her.

"No. Don't! Not yet!" she said, frowning.

"Sorry. Have to give it a rest."

Patrice groaned as Spur disconnected their bodies and sat on his heels between her legs. He ran a hand over his forehead, slicking up sweat. The woman sighed and closed her eyes. "You okay, little lady?"

"I don't think so." Patrice shook her head. "You sure are one hell of a man, Spur! And I do mean man!" She feigned exasperation. "They should hang a sign around your neck warning innocent women to stay away from you."

"Now why would you say a thing like that?" He crossed his arms. "I'm decent and honest and help little old biddies across the street."

"It's your thing! It's so big—bigger than any man

should have the right to have! Spur, I didn't know if I was dying or getting off!"

"If I did have that sign would you have stayed away?" he asked, gazing down at her nude body.

"Heck, Spur, I said *innocent* women."

"Sure am glad you aren't innocent."

She smiled, smug, assured. "Good. Then you won't mind if we do it again?"

He groaned and fell onto her, sending her into a fit of laughter.

6

Jack T. Galde paced in his motel room. The small, sparsely furnished room irritated him, infuriated him. He could be living in a big house instead of being cramped up in this godforsaken dump.

Fury pulsed through him until he finally sighed and sat on the hard wooden chair he'd bought after arriving in town. It couldn't be helped. He couldn't live anywhere else. Vanessa Thompson was firmly ensconced in the parsonage and his subtle hints that he'd like to move in there hadn't made her suddenly offer the place to him.

There he was, in a backwater Kansas town, five thousand dollars richer than he'd been two months ago and yet living in a dingy hotel.

But that was the least of the problems of this job, Galde thought bitterly. Anywhere else he'd gone he could walk into a saloon like any normal man and suck down a bottle of whiskey. He could fool around with the fancy ladies and play some faro without raising an eyebrow.

Here, however, trapped in that damned preacher's outfit, he couldn't move, couldn't eat, couldn't even take a shit without risking offending someone or threatening to expose his disguise for what it was.

He needed a drink. God, he needed a drink. Something to kill his brain for a while, to numb his anger and his unfulfilled lust. Something to make him *human* again.

Sighing, his throat parched and scratchy, Galde leaned back on the hard chair and thought about his position. The people of Holmes had immediately taken to him. Their need for a preacher—a lucky break—had allowed him to assume that role without any problems.

But he suspected that damn widow, Vanessa Thompson, thought something wasn't quite right about him. She watched him everywhere, studied him intently while he preached, even checked his biblical references in church to make sure they were right. A thought gnawed away in his mind. She didn't quite believe him, the little cunt. That could make her dangerous, or at least a problem.

Hell, he'd have to speed up his plan. In just a few days he'd rob the bank and leave town. Flush with all that new wealth, where would he go? He scorned the idea of setting up another job like this one. He needed a break.

Maybe he'd take the train to San Francisco. He'd get a room in the most expensive hotel in town and fill it up with fancy ladies. He'd guzzle whiskey and women until he couldn't see or piss straight.

The thought brought a smile to the pudgy man's lips. Well, hell, maybe it was worth waiting for. Just a few more days. But first . . . he'd better call on Vanessa, assure her of his devotion to God, assuage any doubts that lingered in her holier-than-thou mind.

Jack T. Galde was a simple man. Born of a God-fearing mother and a crabber in a tiny town in Maine, he'd been reared with Bible readings and steaming meals of cracked crab, fish and clam chowder. At first he'd been taken in with the idea of God—a powerful, all-seeing deity who'd strike you down with lightning if you so much as *thought* about a girl in the way you weren't supposed to think.

Soon, however, he started having those thoughts about Mindy, a girl who lived nearby. He thought about what was under her dress and it had made his crotch pound. He thought about what she looked like under all that dark wool.

The more he dwelled on such subjects, the more his mother's Christian teachings slipped away into some deep part of his brain. He'd played with Mindy one cold winter night, sticking his hand between her legs and fingering her. No flash of divine power struck his body, only normal boyish lust. Proving to himself that his mother had been wrong about sex, he'd decided to see what else she'd lied about.

He stole money from the collection plate at church. He lifted pouches of tobacco from old Mr. Dorman's store and rolled his own smokes with newspaper. He finally picked a fight with the town bully who'd terrorized him for years, beating him with his fists until the bloody boy bawled his head off and ran screaming for his mommy.

As he stretched his horizons and grew into young manhood Jack Galde realized that the world was his. He could have anything he wanted. *Anything.* If people wouldn't give it to him, he'd steal it. If they tried to stop him, he'd hurt them.

Nothing was sacred—not women, property or life itself. Galde quickly realized that the small-town surroundings weren't big enough for him, so he left home at fifteen on his father's horse and rode to New York.

Three years in the bowels of that dirty, noisy city turned him into a hardened youth. He had his first woman, tasted his first whiskey, played his first game of poker. He ripped diamond bracelets off fat women's wrists and grabbed purses. Hiding out in abandoned buildings with other thieves and thugs he managed to build a small fortune. Galde outfitted himself in the most expensive clothing (which, uncharacteristically, he bought) and became a full-time thief, earning a tremendous living at the expense of other people. When they gave him trouble he'd flash his gun and they'd relent.

Not long after, he shot his first man. A policeman, responding to a woman's cries for help, ran after him. He dropped her purse and, cursing, turned and fired without even thinking about it. The slug pierced the cop's heart and sent him to the ground, dead.

Excited at the power over life and death in his hands, he gave up simple thievery and let it be

known that he'd kill anyone, anywhere, for a
price. He had many takers among the up and
coming politicians and suited businessmen.

Finally, 15 years of life in New York left him
cold. He headed west and began his new career. At
first he pulled some simple bank robberies with a
few hired guns but he soon bored of that. Three
months spent hitting trains was just as tiring, so he
holed up in St. Louis and invented a new way of
separating people from their money.

At first he'd enjoyed the game he played. He'd
settle down in a new town, earning the people's
trust, drinking and eating with them, becoming a
friendly local.

Then, when the time was right, he'd rob the
bank, kill anyone who tried to stop him and
silently ride out of town. He'd done it five times so
far, pulling off each job without a hitch.

He hadn't been caught. No one suspected him of
his crimes. No sheriffs were staring at wanted
posters that showed his ugly face, no witnesses still
enjoyed the breath they'd need to accuse him.

Galde enjoyed making his mark across the west.
He relished the wide-open spaces after the
deadening darkness of New York City. Moreoover,
the money was easy and there were few lawmen
around to try to stop him. Those few that did exist
didn't have the brains or guts to find him.

Spur slumped onto Patrice, exhausted.

"Come on, honey, again!"

"Hey, I'm not a machine!" He rolled off her. He
stared at the ceiling and squeezed her firm breasts.

"Patrice, you're a hell of a woman. But I gotta rest."

She sighed. "Okay. But promise me this won't be the last time."

"I promise you. Now let me take a nap."

"You're—you're not really here to start a newspaper like you said, are you?" Her voice was hesitant, unsure.

He looked over at her. "What makes you say that?"

She flung yellow hair from her eyes. "I don't know. Just a hunch. My mother, the actress, always used to say that these thoughts came into her head from nowhere. Sometimes it happens to me. And I don't think that's why you're here."

Spur shrugged. "So?"

Patrice sighed. "Okay. So don't tell me. I don't care—really I don't! Just as long as you don't ride out of town tomorrow morning."

"I may be sticking around for a day or two," Spur said, realizing that the young woman's charms had temporarily blotted out all thoughts of his current job.

"You better not leave before I have the chance to give you a going-away present." Patrice wickedly grinned at him.

He moaned. "I've got a hunch what that might be."

She smiled. "See? My mother the *actress* was right!"

Vanessa Thompason walked hurriedly to the door. Who could be knocking at this late hour? She

turned up the kerosene lamps on either side of the
door and opened it.

"Preacher Golden!" she exclaimed. "Praise the
Lord it's you! I was a little worried, being this late
and all. I was just about to retire for the evening."

Galde smiled. "Then I'm glad I'm not unduly
disturbing you, Mrs. Thompson. Can I come in?"

She nodded curiously and stepped back. "What
brings you here at this hour?"

"God, Mrs. Thompson." He settled into one of
the needlepoint covered chairs in the parlor.

"What about Him?"

The preacher was acting more peculiar than
ever, Vanessa thought, as she sat opposite the man.

He looked down in supposed anguish. "I believe
I'm having a crisis of faith."

"Preacher Golden, if that's the case I don't see
why you're talking to me—though I appreciate
your honesty."

"Who else can I turn to but you or God?" He
looked up at her wearily. "Every citizen of Holmes
knows you're the most God-fearing woman
around. But the Lord hasn't answered my
prayers."

She was interested. "What—what *kind* of crisis
are you experiencing?"

"The Fiend in the Bottle calls to me. The Devil
makes me thirst for alcohol."

Relief shot through Vanessa. So he was human
after all. "Preacher Golden, that's not a crisis of
faith; just a hankering after sin. No man's perfect.
Even men of the cloth may drink a bit now and
then. Even Charles—"

"Not I, Mrs. Thompson. I fear the Devil is taking hold of me. But that's not all that I crave. That's not the lowest of the abominations that burn to control my sinful body." He peered into the woman's eyes, gazing at her.

Vanessa grew uncomfortable under his stare. She hadn't seen a man look at her like that since—since her late husband had one of his bouts of fleshy lust.

Lust! She was shocked beyond all words.

"Preacher Golden, I think you'd better go back to your room, get down on your knees and pray to be washed by the blood of Jesus. Confess your sins and you shall be redeemed!"

Galde rose. "How can I confess to evil without trying them out first?"

She sat open-mouthed as he rose and walked over to her, lowering his gaze to her chest.

"Your fine looking titties jutting out like that are driving me crazy! You're a hell of a good looking woman, Vanessa!"

Her face colored. "Get out. Get out! You're no man of God! I knew it the minute I saw you!"

Galde laughed. "Was that the minute I 'answered your prayers?'" He roared with laughter and reached for her breasts with both hands.

She slapped him away, stood and backed against the wooden chair.

"You're in league with the Devil!" Vanessa said, tight-lipped. "Stay away from me!"

"Vanessa! Let me show you the ways of sin! Let us share in the wicked delight of *lust*, my dear!"

"Abomination! Devil! I rebuke you, Satan!" Vanessa stepped backward into the chair, knocking it to the ground and crashing down after it.

She slammed onto the floor. Hurt, stunned, she saw Galde lunge down toward her. Vanessa scrambled to her feet, trying to free herself of the stocky man's grabbing hands as pain shot through her body.

"Come on, Vanessa, you know you want to!"

"No! You speak with the Devil's tongue! Abadon!"

"You're gonna dry up without some good loving in your hole!" Galde slapped her face, leered and ripped the front of her simple black dress, tearing it off at her waist.

Shocked, nude to the waist, Vanessa slapped back. Galde chuckled until she broke free and hurried to the front door. Then he was there, holding the knob firmly, trapping the woman between his arms. She looked up at him, helpless, drained of energy. Her fight had left her.

"If it's God's will. . . ." she said slowly, looking at the floor.

He laughed. "Sorry, honey, I gotta disappoint you. I don't wanna rape you."

"You don't!" Vanessa glanced at his face. "Then why are you doing this?"

"I couldn't control myself. All I want is your money. Frankly, my dear, I don't have the time." He picked the woman up, stumbled once under her weight and carried her into the bedroom. He threw her onto the quilt-covered feathered mattress, stripped off his belt and tied her hands together behind her back.

Vanessa lay in a daze, unable to cope with the

reality of the situation, watching emotionless as Galde stormed through her dresser drawers.

"Nothing. Nothing! Come woman, you must have something worth stealin'!"

Why was this happening to her? Why, Lord why?

"Ah hah! What have we here?"

She stifled a sob as he brought out a small, carved wooden jewelry case. Vanessa's cheeks burned as he opened it. Not that, she thought. Not that!

"All kinds of expensive shit," he mumbled.

Galde removed the strand of pearls her father had given her as a girl; the diamond earrings and emerald brooch, gifts of former suitors; the gold chains and all the other shameful fripperies that she'd stored away after she'd become a preacher's wife because she hadn't had the heart to part with these vestiges of her former life.

The exposure of her long-hidden secrets enraged Vanessa but she was powerless to resist. As much as she bucked on the bed she couldn't release her hands.

"Well well well. Vanessa, you can't be half bad if you've got goodies like these. And I thought you were a woman of God." He stuffed them into his pockets.

"I *am* a woman of God," she said in a low voice. "Just not a perfect one."

He looked around further but, finding nothing else of value, smiled at the bound woman on the bed. "Good day to you, Vanessa. You won't be seeing me again."

"The Lord will punish you for your sins!" she screamed. "He will find you and kill you and cast you into eternal hell-fire, Joshua Golden!"

"I don't think so, but pray to your God that someone finds you soon. Frankly, I don't give a shit." He blew her a kiss and hurried out of the room.

Vanessa pushed her face into the quilts and cried.

Patrice Carlon tip-toed out of her room. She didn't want to wake up the handsome naked man who slept there. Glancing back at Spur, she pulled her shawl tighter around her and closed the door.

After leaving her hotel she walked along in the fresh, chilled air, enjoying it, feeling it clear her mind of the sex-mists that still boiled within it.

She strolled down the short lengths of boardwalk that fronted the town's buildings—the general store, the combination post office and notary public, clothing shop, the milliner's. As she approached the bank Patrice was puzzled by the fact that its front door stood wide-open.

That's strange, she thought, even for a small town like this. Patrice walked up to the bank.

A short man ran out the door, colliding with her, nearly knocking her over and spilling the bag from his hand.

"You! Who are you?" the man asked.

Patrice reeled back. "I—I—"

"Never mind."

Two men approached a block away. The pudgy man glanced at them, then at the girl. "You're coming with me!" He slapped an arm around her head, covered her mouth with his hand and painfully yanked her along with him.

Patrice struggled against his powerful grip as he

dragged her to the horse that waited behind the bank. What in the world was happening?

When they got to the mount the man slapped her cheek hard enough to send her head spinning. She felt herself being lifted onto the saddle, then the man's body pressing against hers.

In seconds they were off and moving across the darkened landscape. The buildings sped past until they had left Holmes and were out into the countryside.

"Where are you taking me?" she asked, afraid.

"Shut up or I'll throw you off!"

Patrice looked down at the dimly-lit ground that raced beneath them, sighed and shook her head. Her mind reeling from fright and pain, Patrice held onto his pudgy sides as the horse whinnied and bolted into the unknown.

7

Spur stirred. A sensuous lethargy filled his long body as he stretched and greeted the dawn. Somewhere outside a bird chirped erratically.

He yawned, coughed, scratched his stubble and reached over to the bed beside him. His hand hit cool sheets. Surprised, he shifted to full consciousness, opened his eyes and blinked. Patrice wasn't there.

Mystified, he glanced around the room. The blonde girl was nowhere in sight. McCoy wiped his eyes, shook his head, stood and dressed a little faster than he normally might have. Not that he had anything to worry about—Patrice had probably gone to breakfast, or out for one of those strolls she said she enjoyed so much.

He stuffed his feet into his boots, slapped on his hat and walked out of the room. Still yawning, Spur did find it a little strange that the woman who'd begged him to do it again and again last night wasn't around the next morning for a repeat performance. He expected her to wake him up with her mouth—below his waist.

Then again, he never really understood women. At least not all women.

He walked out into the blazing Kansan sunshine. The street seemed unusually busy. Perhaps two dozen men crowded around a tall, lean figure. Hal Phillips, Spur thought, the unofficial lawman. Women and children ambled about, two babies screamed, dust filled the air from iron-wrapped wheels and horseshoes.

Dazed by the confusion, Spur stumbled around, looking, listening. What the hell was going on? Shouts echoed through the street but he couldn't make out any of the words.

McCoy grabbed a passing man's shirtsleeve. "Hey! What's all the excitement about?" he asked.

The calico-shirted farmer, clearly irritated at the interruption, wrestled his sleeve from Spur's grip. "Ain't you heard?" he asked testily. "Reverend Joshua Golden tried to rape Vanessa Thompson last night!"

McCoy was stunned. "I don't believe it."

He remembered the Bible-thumping, fat, black-haired, greasy-faced man.

"And that ain't all," he said, wide-eyed. "He tied her up and robbed her."

Spur said, "And that's what kicked up all this commotion?"

"No, asshole!" the wrinkle-faced farmer said, his eyes narrowing. "Then that fine new preacherman of ours robbed the bank and kidnapped that new

girl who works down to the Glittering Garter—"
He shook his head. "What's her name?"

Spur's pulse quickened. "Patrice Carlon?"

"Yep. Then that damned man rode out of town
with the two things dearest to my heart—my
money and a fine piece of woman-flesh!"

"How you know all this?" McCoy asked.
"Anyone see him do it?"

The farmer glanced behind him. "Well, Mrs.
Thompson tole us all about what happened to her
herself. She managed to git her hands untied and
walked outside. She wuz goin' to Hal to tell him
about it when she seed a man barge outa the bank
with a big sack, grab a blonde girl and disappear
out back!"

"And Golden's missing this morning?"

"Yeah, damn straight he's missin'!" The farmer
bolted toward the man who'd earlier accused Spur
of stealing his horse.

"Which way did he ride?" Spur called after the
departing figure.

"Everyone says east. That's what they think!"

Spur shook his head. No way. Joshua Golden—
or whatever his real name was—wouldn't
backtrack. It was too dangerous for a man in his
profession.

Now, too late, it was so clear to him. Golden was
the man who'd pulled the string of bank robberies.
He'd been right under his nose but Spur had barely
noticed him. And now he had Patrice Carlon!

Patrice recoiled from the stench rising from
Golden's armpits but realized she had no choice.
She gripped his waist and hung on. The horse

wasn't galloping and hadn't for several hours, but she was unused to its movements and thought she was in danger of falling to the dirt at any second.

It had been a living nightmare, clutching to the man's broad back for hour after hour, listening to his cheery, foul-mouthed talk, contemplating her possible futures. None of them looked bright.

Why the heck did I have to go on that moonlight walk? The question pounded in her brain until long after the first streaks of dawn had spilled over onto the western horizon ahead of them. She could be snuggled up to the man of her dreams—well, the man of her current dreams—instead of getting her fanny bruised by the uncomfortable, cramped seat she'd been forced to take on a saddle.

"Yeah," Galde said, breaking into her thoughts again. "You just hold tight, blondie. Much as I hate to say it, I'm kinda glad you came along for the ride. You'll be my first woman in—hell, two, three weeks."

The loud smacking noises which issued from Galde's lips turned her stomach. She just didn't know how much more of this she could take. If she couldn't escape—which didn't seem too likely— maybe she could talk him into releasing her.

"You oughta be ashamed of yourself, hiding your thieving ways behind the Bible! I still can't believe you fooled all those people into thinking you were a preacher."

"Hell, I fooled you. Filled you with fire and brimstone until you couldn't stand to be near me. I'm a good actor." Galde chuckled at the statement.

"No you're not!" Patrice hissed, batting swirling

dust from before her eyes. "My mother's a great actress in St. Louis. She'd probably kick you out of any show you were in. You're just a thief, a common thief."

He reigned in the horse to a stop. Jack T. Galde looked over his shoulder at her. "There ain't nothing common about me, blondie. 'Cept maybe my lustings." He grinned evilly at her, showing broken, yellowed teeth. "I got a pow'rful lusting that's just itching to be satisfied."

Patrice shivered and looked away from his eyes. "It's time you let me go."

He laughed and kicked the horse to a fast walk, ignoring the woman's words.

Goldwater—named after the muddy river that ran straight through the town—was right where Marshal Porter had indicated it would be on his map. It was a rude, growing settlement of about fifty people and half as many buildings. Spur knew it was too small a place for Golden to stop in for more than resupplying.

He rubbed down his foaming horse and let it drink from a slightly green trough as he asked around about a stocky man and a young, blonde-haired woman. The townsfolk he met were uncommunicative but few seemed alarmed or interested in his words.

One old man, sitting in a rocking chair in the shade of the barber shop, summed it up: "Hell, ain't been no excitement around here for years. Sorry, feller! Your two little love-birds didn't fly into here last night or this morning."

Frustrated, Spur questioned several more people

and then tried his luck at two of the outlying farms. The first one, slightly off the trail from Holmes, was unproductive. The second one was abandoned —the windmill flying six broken vanes, bales of hay rotting in the sun, a dead horse lying in the middle of the yard.

Unwilling to waste more time, Spur trusted to his instincts. It wasn't a coincidence. Golden was the man who'd robbed the other banks and he was headed onto the next—with the girl who'd shared her bed with him last night.

He rode west, pushing his horse.

"I keep telling you, blondie; you're too dangerous. So shut your pretty little mouth and let me do some thinking!"

"Don't strain yourself." Patrice laughed, staring at the back of his narrow-brimmed black hat. "Honestly, the way you talk you'd think I was an armed criminal or something. I'm just a young girl in a very strange part of the country. How could I possibly be dangerous to you?"

He grunted. "You won't talk me into letting you go. Now or ever."

Patrice hung onto her hope. She figured he'd only take her part of the way out of town and leave her somewhere to fend for herself. "But you've got a headstart! And no one'll ever find you!"

"You're right about that. No one *ever* finds me. But that's still not a good enough reason to let you go. You're too pretty to leave here out in the middle of nowhere." He reached behind him, grabbed her hand and dragged it forward.

Patrice squirmed as he pressed it into his fat

crotch. She slapped his back and jerked her hand free. "You animal!" she said, her cheeks coloring. Then she calmed down. As much as it made her ill to think of it, she did have another bargaining tool. It was the most expensive commodity a woman owned.

"Mr. Golden—"

"The name's Galde. Jack T. Galde."

"Whatever! Mr. Galde, if—if I let you have me, you know—in *that* way—"

"You mean *fuck* you?" He grunted.

"Yes."

"Stick it in your pussy and slam it in and out?"

"Yes!"

"Bank your tight little hole until I shoot my—"

"Yes! Yes!" She sighed at his colorful description. "If I let you do that to me, then you'd let me go. Right? I mean, then you'd have everything you want and I wouldn't be any more use to you. Why don't you just stop this smelly old horse? Let's get together for a while."

His laugh was short, harsh. "Hell, I was planning on fucking you anyway. If you're even half-good I'm not fool enough to let you out of my sight. I'll fuck you for five or six days at least."

Her throat tightened. "And then?"

He laughed. "Probably won't kill you. You're too pretty to kill, with all that blonde hair."

She shut her eyes. At least that's one thing she didn't have to worry about. Patrice picked a grain of dirt from her lips. "Then how about money? I could pay you any amount you want."

Galde was silent for a moment. "How much?"

"I—I don't know. A hundred dollars?"

He guffawed. "Hell, woman I ain't counted it yet but I must've taken ten thousand dollars from that piss-poor Holmes bank! Just sit tight, blondie. We'll stop soon enough and rustle up some grub."

"Stop calling me that!" she said with sudden violence. "My name's Patrice!"

"Sure, blondie. Sure." He guffawed as they rode through the bleak, flat landscape.

The trail between Goldwater and Fagan showed many deep ruts caused by the passage of carriages and stagecoaches, as well as countless horseshoe impressions formed in earlier, wetter months. Spur stopped and studied them at regular intervals, allowing his mare to rest, but couldn't make out any regular tracks that would positively tell him that he was going the right way.

As he rode, exasperated, McCoy kept telling himself that the man may have bypassed Goldwater but probably wouldn't ride through Fagan. The town was much larger. He was sure that if he didn't find him on the trail, he'd find Golden in Fagan.

A thief like him didn't suddenly alter his plan. That was the only thing he had going for him. That, and a hunch. Spur smiled as he remembered Patrice using that word, remembering her warmth, her scent, her lust.

The thoughts quickly dissolved into a sense of urgency. If he wasn't careful all he'd have of her were memories.

"Come on, girl, faster!" Spur yelled, gently stroking the mare's flanks with his boots, urging her toward the man and woman whom he knew were ahead of him.

Patrice sat on the sand, legs crossed beneath her, her arms bound behind her back with a short piece of stiff rope. It bit into her wrists every time she tried to move them into a comfortable position but the young woman soon decided that she wouldn't notice the pain, wouldn't occupy her thoughts with anything but her biggest problem—how she was going to get away from Jack Galde.

She thought vainly of Spur McCoy, the man she'd left behind. When he woke up and noticed that she was gone, would he look for her? Would he hear about her kidnapping? Did anyone know about it? Would Spur ride out and try to save her from this smelly man? Or would he simply carve another notch on his belt and get on with his life?

She didn't know him well enough to decide.

Across from her in the primitive campsite he'd carved out in the midst of a copse of cottonwoods, Jack T. Galde threw more kindling on the fire he'd built. The dry wood caught quickly, flashing into a brilliant, temporary blaze that died down as he stuffed larger branches into it.

He went through his saddlebags and produced a coffee pot, some coffee and a bit of hardtack. Galde glanced over at the woman and smiled.

"Gourmet eats."

She sniffed at him. "I'm not gonna eat a thing," Patrice said, and turned her head from the man. "You'd probably try to poison me."

"No way. Too much of a waste." He settled down before the fire.

"And anyway, I thought you were gonna rape me. How come you're suddenly more hungry than horny?" Not that she wanted him to, of course; it was just something to irritate him with. Maybe if he got mad enough at her, he'd leave her behind.

Galde laughed. "So you *do* want it! I thought so the minute I saw you walking in town. Had the hots for me as a preacher and still have 'em for me as a thief! You want me bad, don't you, blondie?"

"Not on your life!" Patrice shook her head. "But, I mean, after all those weeks without a woman, I just figured—well, heck, I don't think you can."

He grunted. "Can what?"

"You know! Maybe you like horses."

"Hell, you're jealous of that beast? You're a strange little woman, blondie."

"Patrice!" she said hotly. "My name's Patrice!"

"Sure. Sure, blondie."

She blew out her breath. At least he hadn't hurt her or tried to rape her—yet. But Patrice had this sinking feeling that despite the man's words, despite his reassurances, he'd either use her and kill her, or simply kill her.

The thought wasn't comforting, so Patrice blocked it out by intently watching Galde filling the coffeepot with water from the dented canteen.

It could be lots worse, she thought. He could be filling *her*.

8

Spur rode for most of the day, following the invisible tracks that he was sure were there on the trail. Well after noon the steel rails of the railroad sidled up beside him, stretching out like giant, dark-scaled snakes.

The endless acres of rich cropland and their attendant farm houses and barns, as well as a few scattered ranches, gave way to open land. Not long after riding through cultivated areas, the burgeoning town of Fagan, Kansas, rose before him.

Moving into it, Spur was impressed with the place. Two-story brick buildings as well as wooden structures lined the eight main streets. As he passed three hotels, the bank, the city hall and five saloons—as well as a variety of dry-goods stores—he was startled at the town's appearance. Everything looked fresh, new, well-kept.

Hundreds of people crowded the streets, vying for space with carriages and horses of every description. The train had apparently just stopped at the Fagan station, leaving in its wake a new load of confused, belongings-loaded men, women and children standing in Fagan with their hopes and dreams.

It had grown in a few short years from an isolated crossroads to a full-fledged town. The coming of the railroad had brought with it a steady influx of city dwellers ready to eke their livings from the verdant topsoil in the surrounding countryside.

Once there they bought precious lumber, nails, barrels, wagons, cloth, horses, pots and pans, food, kerosene and all manner of life necessities before striking out to find their own piece of land.

The noise surrounding him was almost deafening. From the blacksmith came the clanging of ironwork. A group of pigs squealed as they were led by an eldery, humpbacked man. Dozens of children screamed and cried to their parents. Carriages clattered by and horses whinnied. From within the saloons a cacaphony of off-key piano music mixed with the sound of drunkards demanding more whiskey.

Saddle-weary, caked with dust and thirsty, Spur rode into Fagan. The size of the town and the activity that seethed in it made it seem rather unlikely for Golden's purposes—too large, too many people, too many possible witnesses for him to pull off the kinds of bank robberies he was used to.

However, Spur knew—*knew*—that the man had

come here and, he hoped, had brought Patrice with him. The dear girl, Spur thought. Why had she gone out that night? Would she still be back in Holmes, fending off groping cowboys and kicking her beautiful legs into the air in the Glitter Garter Saloon, if he'd just done it a third time with her?

He shook off the thought. Too late for that now. And besides, like he'd told her, he was only human. He had his limitations.

Spur tied his horse up before the National Hotel —the best looking of the ones he'd seen after riding through half the town—and registered. The price was slightly higher than he was used to but money wasn't of any importance. In his room he threw his carpetbag onto the sturdy bed and was surprised that it actually bounced. Maybe he'd get a good night's sleep.

By the time he'd finished scraping off several layers of trail dirt and donned a fresh change of clothing, the sun had set. He grabbed dinner and went upstairs. McCoy stopped by at the unmanned front desk and flipped through the register. No familiar names—such as Golden—had been recorded in the last day.

He went outside to find Golden, Patrice—or, preferably, both of them.

Even after dark, Buttonwood Street was alive with people. Young as well as old lovers walked hand-in-hand. Men streamed in and out of the ever-busy saloons. Fancy ladies daringly walked the boardwalk alone, wrapped in tight dresses that picked up the light of exterior kerosene lamps that lined the street in all the right places.

It would be fruitless to search every male face in the hopes of finding Joshua Golden—or whatever his name was. But there were always the saloons. If any of them had dancing girls, and if Patrice had made it this far—

He checked all five. Two offered shows—the Horseshoe and the Red Ace. He watched the women go through their contortions in the first saloon but Patrice certainly wasn't among them. The 'girls' were well into their thirties and beyond, and their talent lay on their chests and between their legs—certainly not in them.

He walked into the Red Ace just as the show was ending to a rip-roaring ovation from the appreciative, liquor-laced male audience. From the back of the saloon McCoy thought he saw Patrice just before the blonde-haired girl turned and ran backstage with the other five women.

If he wasn't mistaken, she was in Fagan. His mind raced. Had she been kidnapped? Of course. She wouldn't have left her clothing behind had she simply decided to leave Holmes. And if she was there, was Joshua Golden there as well?

Remembering a stage door in the alley beside the building, Spur went outside and waited there. Several other young women, in pairs or accompanied by men he assumed were Red Ace employees, left through the door. Finally, Patrice walked out, her face flushed. She'd changed into a simple green dress.

"Patrice!" Spur said.

The woman stared at him in fright, rigid for five seconds before melting and running to him. She hugged him, pressing her face into his neck. "Spur McCoy! I thought I'd never see you again!" she said.

"Likewise." He gripped her waist as hard as he dared. "You seem healthy enough, Patrice. What the hell are you doing in Fagan?"

She broke from him. "It's a long story." The blonde looked up at him with sad eyes. "Jack Galde—that's Joshua Golden's real name—kidnapped me the other night after we'd—well, you know. I just happened to be going by the bank on my stroll while he was robbing it.

"I tried to get him to let me go but he wouldn't. Nothing I did or said would convince him otherwise. And he kept threatening to rape me." She made a face.

"Did he?"

"No. That's the funny thing about it. He had every opportunity to but he never did. Maybe I was right, maybe he only likes horses."

Spur smirked at her.

Patrice sighed. "So, yesterday afternoon, he finally stopped his horse and let me off. He said I was filling his mind with all sorts of crazy thoughts and he needed to think straight right then. I think he just couldn't stand to have me around any more. I'm afraid I talked him half out of his mind." She smiled, curling up her lips in a delicious grin. "Jack told me to go back to Holmes but it seemed too far. I'd heard him talking about Fagan, and even saw a map of his one time showing where it was, and so I headed here. My feet are still hurting."

"And got a job dancing?"

She nodded. "Mr. Weatherby had an opening

and so I was on stage less than an hour after I straggled in. I was dancing before I'd even gotten a hotel room—bruised feet and everything. After all, I didn't have a dime on me. No money, no clothes, nothing. And besides—Mr. Weatherby pays twice as much as I was making in Holmes. And here we're just dancers—nothing else.'' She raised her eyebrows suggestively.

"I see. Have you see this Jack Galde since?''

Patrice frowned. "I didn't until just tonight. He came in during our first number. I was mortified when he noticed me, wondering what he'd do. Though he'd let me go, I'm sure he didn't expect to see me here. I waited around backstage until I finally had to leave.'' She looked at him fondly. "You have no idea how happy I was to see you out here—instead of that man.''

Spur nodded. "So he's here. Somewhere in this mass of people.'' He paused. "Did Galde say what he was doing next? Was he planning on robbing the bank here too?''

"I—I don't think so. He said something about 'laying low' for a while. Seems he's got plenty of money to spend.''

"Makes sense. I didn't think he'd try anything here. It's not his style.''

Patrice glanced around. "Look, Spur, I'd love to talk to you some more, but not here. I—I can feel him out there. Just knowing that he's in the same town is enough to give me the creeps.'' She shivered.

Spur gave her his arm. "Your room or mine?'' he asked.

"It doesn't matter to me,'' she said, taking it.

They walked off.

Jack T. Galde stared at the Red Ace Saloon from
his hotel room window. The show should be over
any minute now, he thought, fingering the pearl
buttons that ran down the front of his red shirt.

Soon, Patrice and some man he vaguely
recognized from Holmes emerged from the alley
beside the saloon and strolled off, arm in arm.

He scowled. Never should have let her go, he
thought. Never leave any loose ends that can come
back and trip you up just when you thought everything was going fine. He should've killed her the
minute he stumbled into her as he was leaving the
bank. Hell, he'd killed lots of women before. One
more wouldn't have made much difference one
way or the other.

But when he recognized her face, saw the
shimmering blonde hair, he made a snap decision
and dragged her along with him. He was aching for
female companionship and all the charms that
were at their disposal and thought that, if nothing
else, she could give it to him. And besides, those
men were walking up.

After a few hours, though, he realized that what
had attracted him to her in the first place soon
repelled him. The golden mane, the high, youthful
voice all reminded him of one lady, the woman
who had haunted him for all of his adult life.

His mother.

He slammed his fist onto the windowsill, making
a long red mark across his knuckles. The pain was
good, Galde thought, and he repeated the motion.

Agony set his mind in motion, got his head clear of stupid feelings.

He remembered his early adoration of his mother, that woman who'd had her nose stuck in the Good Book for so long that she'd never thought to take it out and look at the real world. He remembered how he'd idolized her until he'd realized that while God was fine for those interested in storing up for the life after death—if it did exist—life itself was the most important thing. He'd decided to wring as much out of it as he could.

However, the image of his mother—with her serene, almost simple face, high cheekbones and ringlets of hair the exact shade of daffodils—had stayed with him. Sometimes, as he lay panting beside a nameless whore while bad whiskey lubricated his brain, he thought of her, remembering the pretty woman she'd been. The thoughts bothered him, angered him.

Patrice soon did the same to him. However, he just couldn't kill her, not the way she looked. As much as he despised her smart, ever-running mouth, she was too beautiful a woman to waste. So he'd dumped her in the countryside between the two small towns, hoping she'd either die out there by herself or head back to Holmes. Either way, he assumed he'd never see the blonde bitch again.

Now, her sudden appearance in Fagan presented a problem to him. Patrice was dangerous, very dangerous. She knew far too much about him, enough to get him either lynched or legally kicking in the wind. All she had to do was go and spill the details to the local law.

Galde rubbed his head. It was too early to move on. He had plenty of money to spend and Fagan was a comfortable enough town. It was also big enough that he could blend in without being noticed—as long as no loose ends were dangling around.

He felt fury boil in his gut. He should've killed her then and there and been done with it. Never too late to settle unfinished business. This time he wouldn't let his feelings get in the way.

He slammed his knuckles onto the windowsill again.

He'd kill her. Kill the little bitch with the big mouth. Kill her before she killed him.

"Good evening, Miss Carlon," the craggy-faced man in an expensive New York suit said from the front register in the Crouching Lion Hotel.

"Good even, Peter." She walked into the fairly elegant lobby with Spur by her side.

"I enjoyed the show last night. You're very good." The beady-eyed man stared at her with admiration well mixed with hunger.

"Thank you, Peter." Patrice smiled at Spur as they walked to the stairs.

"It's a pleasure to have you staying here."

She giggled as they rose and burst into laughter on the landing.

"What's wrong with you?" McCoy asked.

"See why I like staying here? Back in Holmes I was a whore. Vanessa Thompson said it to my face. Here I'm a *star*, just like my mother always said I'd be."

She extracted a shining skeleton key from the small beaded purse that hung on her left shoulder and quickly opened her room.

Spur was impressed by its size and furnishings. This was no cheap hotel, judging from the cut-crystal lamps, the lace doilies that topped two cherrywood tables and the huge bed covered with thick woolen blankets.

Patrice threw her purse onto the bed and lit the small table-top lamp that stood before the window. She reached in through the curtains and opened it. A light breeze blew the filmy material into the air. Patrice turned to McCoy and smiled. ''So, you can see I'm doing well enough here in Fagan.''

''Yes,'' he said, looking around. ''Pretty impressive. There's just one problem.''

''What's that?'' Patrice asked.

''Galde's in town.''

The young woman's happiness melted into a frown. ''Heck. I'd almost forgotten about him. You're right, of course. I should have expected to see him. But when I looked out into the saloon and saw him sitting there, staring at him, I was petrified. Nearly fell off the stage.''

''You had every right to be. Who knows what's going on in his mind? Maybe he's thinking that letting you go wasn't such a good idea.''

She shivered. ''Don't even talk like that. With any luck, he'll be gone from here by tomorrow and I'll never have to see him again.''

''I don't think so,'' he said, walking to her. ''Galde said he'd be laying low. That sounds like sticking around in town for a week or so.''

She looked at him curiously as he approached

her. "You seem awfully interested in him. Was—
was he why you were in Holmes?" she suddenly
asked.

He shrugged. "Could be."

"Damn you, Spur McCoy!" She moved laterally
away from him and stood before the bed, shaking
her head. "You're such a mysterious man. I can't
get you to tell me anything." She huffed, then
purposefully looked at him. Her blue eyes picked
up the light reflecting from the prismed kerosene
lamp. "So let's stop talking, okay? After all, you
still owe me that third one."

He grinned. "Well, if you insist."

"I insist all right."

"Well, then. . . ."

"And I promise not to run off in the middle of the
night. I'm through with my moonlight strolls.
Besides, it'll get that darn man out of my mind for
awhile and do us both a lot of good."

As he went to her again, loud male voices issued
up from the street below. The conversation was
heated, angry. Spur ignored it and touched her
shoulder. Her skin was as soft as a duck's back, he
thought, as a gunshot thundered up into her room.

"What was that?" Patrice asked, freezing up
under his stroking hand.

"Just a fight outside." Spur nuzzled her warm
neck, drinking in the expensive perfume that
lingered there. He nibbled gently on her ear.

"But they might be killing each other! Maybe—
maybe it's not just a fight." Patrice moaned.

"Forget about it."

Nibble. Lick.

"Maybe it's Jack Galde robbing the bank!"

Another shot.

"Don't worry about that. We've got other things to think about."

She shook her head. "If nothing else, I'm closing the window. I can't stand hearing that noise!" Patrice broke from him and went to it.

A third gunshot rocked the night. The window shattered, sending deadly shards of glass against the curtains. At the same instant the kerosene lamp exploded. The burst was short but long fingers of liquid fire spread across the table and fell onto the carpeted floor.

"Christ!" McCoy yelled as the flames rose higher in front of the window and Patrice's scream was nearly drowned out by the screech of broken glass crashing to the floor.

9

Thick smoke curled up to the ceiling. The room brightened as flames licked along the floor and gnawed at the cherrywood table. Patrice stood frozen amid the fire as it howled and snapped around her.

Spur grabbed the woman and threw her onto the bed. Stepping around the blaze, he ripped down the curtains and slapped them at the flames, quenching small portions of them but fanning others.

The fire continued to spread. Cursing, coughing and ignoring the itching in his eyes, McCoy knocked over the table, grabbed up the yet untouched end of the oval rug and roughly folded it in half. As that portion of the fire died out, the curtains combusted. Fire licked the wallpaper.

Spur glanced around, bolted for the pitcher and

dumped its liquid contents onto the flames. They sizzled and sputtered out.

Sighing, he turned around. Patrice sat up on the bed, back straight, her face calm. She folded her hands in her lap but didn't look at him as she spoke. Tears ran down her eyes in the now darkened room. Fresh air blew in from the broken window and swirled out the noxious fumes.

"That was Jack Galde," she said, ghostly in the smoke. "You were right. He's trying to kill me."

Spur went to her. "You don't know that. It could have been a stray shot from the fight in the street." He paused. "But even if it wasn't, you can't stay here. You better spend the night in my room."

Patrice glanced at him and nodded. "Okay." She was still pale.

"Just in case that bullet was meant for you, I don't think it would be a good idea for you to be seen outside right now. Any ideas?"

The question seemed to bring her back to life. Patrice rose and strode to a large trunk near the basin. "Something in here might help. It's a bunch of costumes that Mr. Weatherby lent me to use in the show. Everything just about fits me." She rummaged through it for a few minutes and soon held up a plain black dress, shawl and bonnet. "Will this do?"

McCoy nodded.

Five minutes later Spur left her hotel room and casually walked half a block down from the Crouching Lion. Not long afterward he saw a woman leave the hotel. She was dressed in black, a shawl pulled tightly around her face, her hair

invisible beneath the bonnet. The figure hobbled
along toward the National Hotel, looking for all the
world to be an old, lame woman.

He followed her from a suitable distance, incon-
spicuously glancing around to be sure no one else
was showing any interest in Patrice.

She soon disappeared inside the National. He
hurried after her and joined her in front of his
room. Once inside, Patrice threw off the bonnet
and laughed at McCoy as he turned up the lamps.

"How exciting!" she said as she unwrapped the
shawl and ran her fingers through her hair. "Did I
give a convincing performance?"

He nodded. "You didn't attract any attention.
You were perfect." Spur kissed her nose.

She murmured and touched his shoulders. "Care
to help an old lady out of her clothes?"

He feigned disinterest. "Hell, I don't know,
ma'am. Why, you're old enough to be my—my—"

She playfully punched his chin. "I'm old enough,
all right! Just help me out of these crinolines. I'll
show you how old I am!"

He unbuttoned and unsnapped. The tired, stiff
dress fell to the floor. Though he'd seen her in the
same condition only minutes before, Spur admired
Patrice in a new light as she stood before him
dressed only in petticoats and a thin chemise. Her
skin was as white as her undergarments.

"Anything else I can help you with?"

She smiled and lifted her hands above her head.

Spur gripped the bottom hem of the chemise and
raised it slowly. It revealed a flat stomach and
pouting belly button. Patrice giggled as he bent and
slapped a kiss on it. Raising his head once again he

lifted the chemise higher, exposing her delicious breasts.

"You got a helluva nice pair there, grandma." He acknowledged each nipple with a slick, fast suck. Patrice moaned and writhed as he pulled the chemise past her head and off her arms.

Spur knelt before her, gazing up at her breasts before lowering her petticoat. She kicked it off. Underneath it, another layer of soft cloth still hid what he wanted to see so he removed that too, revealing yet another petticoat. The hunger built within him. He ripped the flimsy material in his haste, finally sending it to the floor.

Her thighs were silken marble—perfect, unblemished, curved in all the right places. Between them, a hand's width below her navel, a patch of blonde hair beckoned him.

Patrice stood naked before him—unashamed, unabashed—an alive and sensual woman. Looking down at him, she held out her arms. Spur rose and locked her in a tight embrace. Her breasts crushed against his powerful chest and their mouths sought out each other, lips parting, tongues clashing. She slipped off his hat.

Without breaking their oral contact, Spur unbuttoned his shirt, wriggled out of it, and then kicked off his boots. Her hands beat his to his fly. Twenty fingers pulled, prodded, pressed and finally managed to free the cloth flap from its prison. Plunging his tongue in and out of Patrice's warm mouth Spur lowered his pants and underdrawers.

He moaned as her hand touched his stiffening penis. Her cool fingers slid around it, gripping him in an erotic embrace. His groin boiled as the woman's touch stroked him, encouraged him and soon worked its magic.

Patrice slid her mouth from his and dropped to her knees. She gazed at the erection that jutted out from his hairy crotch precisely before her eyes. She licked her lips.

"Patrice, you don't have to—" His voice was husky.

"Have to? I *want* to. I've wanted to ever since I saw it!" Her head moved forward. Her lips parted.

Spur felt his knees threaten to give out as liquid heat engulfed him. He steadied himself by placing a hand on her shoulder. The sensations were overwhelming, overpowering, as they flooded through his body.

Hot. Tight. Soft. Demanding. The warmth moved down, farther and farther, her lips sliding along his shaft. Spur stared down at the woman in disbelief, shaking his head as lust shot out from his crotch and spread through his body.

Her head moved up, then down; up, down. Soon blonde hair flew in the air as Patrice hungrily worked him over with her mouth, drawing it deeper into her, embracing it with her tongue, welcoming it.

She pulled off and stared up at him, her eyes glazed, her lips shining. "Grab my head and make me do it!" the panting woman said.

He covered her pink ears with his hands and gently slid back into her. She moaned as she took him. McCoy pushed slowly into her yielding mouth, luxuriating in the silky feeling.

The tension in his groin mounted. He increased

the speed, slipping faster into her, moving her eager head to meet his thrusts.

Deep. Deeper. He felt Patrice's throat relaxing, opening, accepting him until his scrotum slapped against her chin.

It was too much for him to handle. He quickly pulled out of her and stepped back, gasping, his penis trembling, shining in the golden kerosene light.

"What's wrong?" Patrice asked, looking up at him. "Don't you like it?"

"No. I mean, nothing's wrong. It's just, ah, a little too soon for that."

She smiled and jumped to her feet, sending her breasts bouncing. "Then let's move on to the second course. Whaddya say, lover boy?"

He grabbed her and lifted her from the floor. Three steps took them to the bed. After laying the woman on the light pink blankets, Spur stepped between her legs and knelt. He touched her knees and spread them.

"You *have* to," Patrice said with a wry smile.

He glanced up at her and pushed his face into her mystery. The young woman sighed as his red moustache meshed with her soft pubic hair and his tongue licked, tasted, probed.

Her musk set him on fire. He spread her lips and tongued her tight button, flicking back and forth, up and down. Patrice squirmed on the bed and moaned as he pleasured her. Sucking, nibbling, licking, he sent her on a ride into ecstasy that tortured her to a shuddering, shrieking orgasm.

"Spur!" she cried.

Merciless, he did it again, tonguing her to a second climax seconds after the first had subsided. Patrice locked her thighs around his head as she trembled and bucked and rode out the exquisite moment of pleasure.

"Not again!" she said, gasping, puffing. "Please, Spur, mercy!"

She relaxed her legs. McCoy straighened up and gripped the base of his penis. He moved forward as the woman stared into his eyes. She shivered. He plunged, all at once, driving into her, filling her up with his lust.

Their bodies joined in a primal dance. He withdrew and slammed back in, groaning, gripping her shoulders. Patrice undulated beneath him as she accepted his thrusts. Each withdrawal seemed to make her hungrier for the next.

Their heated bodies rocked together in a steady, slow rhythm. Spur sucked in her left breast, forcing it into his mouth as he continued to pound into her. The soft flesh was delicious, warm. He moved up on it and teethed the nipple, gently digging into it. Patrice grabbed his head and forced it down, directing him to chew harder.

He switched to her other mound and worshipped it. Patrice groaned as McCoy stimulated her all over again. He never let up on his steady pumping, sliding in and out of her with primal urgency.

He popped his mouth off her breast and lifted himself onto his hands.

"Oh god, Spur," Patrice said. "Just fuck me."

He grunted and pounded into her, quickening his thrusts, driving into her yielding body with ever-demanding urgency. Unsatisfied unless he fulfilled her needs, Spur moved his body higher until his penis rubbed against her clitoris. Patrice grabbed his pumping buttocks and forced him deeper, faster, harder until their crotches banged together and the bed creaked beneath them.

"Jesus, Patrice!" Spur said as sweat flowed off his body.

Her face took on a new glow. Her mouth opened in a soundless cry, breasts flushing, body trembling, muscles tightening around his shaft.

The increased pressure inside her sent Spur into a frenzy. He bucked and pumped and rammed until the bed banged against the wall, the world went black, his body exploded, and he felt his seed shooting, squirting, rushing into her opening in mindless ecstasy.

Drained, spent, emptied, Spur slid down onto the panting woman, burying his face into her slick breasts, gripping her shoulders, hugging her until his body shook off the powerful release. Patrice patted his hair, stroking it, murmuring soothing words as he slowly regained his senses.

Soon afterward he lifted his head. Haggard, dazed, he looked up at Patrice. The woman's face wavered until his glazed eyes adjusted and sharpened the image. When he saw her clearly, Patrice was smiling at him, radiating joy and fulfillment.

He grinned momentarily and flopped back down onto her breasts.

Stupid! Stupid! Galde stormed around in his room. It had been a stupid idea, stupidly planned, stupidly executed. His face burned as he thought of what his old friends back in New York would say if they knew how he'd bungled the simple job.

Now it was clear. He should have waited until the right moment, not gone tearing off into the night with his rifle, blasting into the empty-headed bitch's room, hoping he'd blow off her face.

Galde remembered how he'd waited, crouched on the roof of the building opposite the Crouching Lion Hotel, watching, waiting until the right moment. Then the fight broke out and he saw his opportunity, but had missed his shot. He was sure that all he'd done was start a fire and clue the blonde woman—and the man he'd seen through the shattered window—to his plans. A stupid mistake.

He tipped up a bottle of whiskey and swallowed down the burning, smoke-flavored liquid. Three gulps later he set the bottle on the table and snarled. The alcohol flowed through him, cobwebbed those parts of his being that he didn't want to face.

You're losing it, Galde, he thought. You're losing your touch. Maybe it's time you quit the business and opened up a whorehouse.

Hell, getting soft on the yellow-haired girl and then letting his anger rule his actions wasn't like him at all. Was it the pressure of his last job, all that Bible-spouting that had mixed him up?

Galde smiled. Yeah. That must've been it. He was okay, stronger than ever, and had enough money to ride out a few weeks more in Fagan.

So he'd kill the girl right, once and for all, and

wait until he saw where the wind took him.

As long as it wasn't hanging from the end of a rope he'd be happy.

10

"You ain't going nowhere, boy!"

The crowd of Fagan newcomers parted down the middle of the street, allowing the passage of a speeding, red-faced youth closely followed by a burly man, Winchester in hand, eyes snarling. Thick, curly black hair stuck out from the bull-necked gunman. His clothes were tattered and caked with dirt.

Looks like trouble, McCoy thought, seconds before the young, pimple-faced buck slammed into him, stared into his face with surprise, stiffened and sighed as he heard the approaching man.

"Johnson! I warned you time and again. Keep your dirty paws off my daughter!"

"But Mr. Salt, I—we—"

"Shut up! But did you listen? No. You let your hot blood get the best of you! Now she's good for nothing, shamed, used like a goddamned whore!

You made her unfit for any upstanding man in this great country of ours! I'll have to put Missy out to pasture with the cows!''

Spur pushed the boy from him. If it got too dangerous he'd step in and try to straighten things out.

Johnson turned around, trembling, eyes lowered to the ground as he faced his enemy.

''Gee. Mr.Salt, I—I didn't mean nothing' by it. Just havin' a little fun.''

Enoch Salt lined up his rifle with the face that pitched before him. ''What the hell you mean by that? You sure as shit meant something by it!'' He puffed in rage.

''But we—''

''You got two choices, Johnson!'' he barked, cutting off the youth's words. ''Marry my Missy— right now. Take her to the preacher and get it done up all legal like. Or give me three bucks.''

The boy was startled. ''Three bucks? What in heck for?'' he asked.

''So I can get you *buried* after I blow your guts into the street! Don't want you stinking up the place!''

''Hey, Enoch, Myers charges five for a box and a plantin'. Price just went up,'' a man called from the crowd that had gathered around to enjoy the confrontation.

''I didn't say *properly* buried!'' he thundered.

''Daddy!'' a thin, high voice said, followed by the appearance of a plain-faced girl. She frowned as she pushed through the people and walked up to Salt. ''Really, daddy! You're shaming me in front of all these people! How dare you? Why don't you just get on back to the ranch!''

"*I'm* shaming *you*?'' He grunted. "Looks like Johnson here already took care of that.''

"You don't understand,'' she began.

"The hell I don't!''

"It isn't what you think. Nothing happened!'' Missy said, grabbing her father's thick arm, trying to lower his aim. "I already told you nothing happened!''

Enoch glanced at his daughter. "Don't try to protect your lover now. Too late for that, Missy.''

The girl violently shook her head. "I'm not protecting him and he's not my lover. Use your head for a change, daddy!''

"My head, huh?'' he said, still glaring at the young man. "Girl, you waltzed into the house a half hour ago with a smile on your face and a rip in your dress. You'd been out walking with Johnson in the woods. I don't see how there's any other explanation.''

"You would if you'd only stopped and listened,'' the horse-faced girl said. "Tommy and I were out walking. I tripped and fell. My dress caught on a stick and that's what tore it up.'' She turned to Johnson. "Tommy was nice enough to help me up. So I gave him a kiss on the cheek. That's all that happened. I swear it! You're just making things up in your mind. You don't trust me. Just because mom ran off with that—''

"It's true!'' Tom Johnson said. He took a step forward. "Look, Salt; I've put up with your bellowing and your thundering and your bullshit for far too long. I'm tired of being accused of things I ain't even done, tired of having to get Missy back home before it gets dark, tired of you and your big mouth!''

Salt puffed, blinked his eyes, stared at the boy and slowly lowered his rifle. ''Well—'' he stammered.

Missy went to the youth. ''You tell him, Tommy!'' Her eyes shined.

''And—and as much as it would hurt my pride to have you as my father-in-law, if you weren't such a foul-minded man I'd ask your daughter to marry me!''

Missy gasped and kissed his cheek.

Enoch Salt pondered for a minute, chewing on his lower lip, then laid his rifle against his shoulder. He shrugged. ''Well, hell, boy; if you're man enough to stand up to me, I guess you're man enough to marry my Missy.'' He grunted again and turned to head for home. ''And Johnson!''

''Yes sir?'' the boy instantly responded.

''You have my daughter back by—by—'' The big man faltered. ''By ten. Ten o'clock!''

Tom smiled. ''Okay—*dad*.''

Spur shook his head and walked away from the little scene, leaving the two young people to carve out their life together.

He continued on his rounds, checking the local hotel registries for recent arrivals. The first three had none that sounded familiar, but the fourth— The Jason Lomax Inn (Fine European Appointments, the sign said)—had one ''Jake Gould'' registered in room 305. That could be Galde, Spur thought. Same initials.

He memorized the room number and walked back outside into the hot sun. Spur moved down to

Patrice's ex-hotel. He studied the buildings that sat opposite from it. Murphy's General Store was directly across. The building's gabled roof seemed tall enough. Galde could have climbed to the roof and easily shot into Patrice's window. Hmmmmmm.

Still unsure if it had been a stray bullet that started the fire, as he'd told the girl to reassure her, or if Galde was indeed bent on killing Patrice, Spur went to the sheriff's office.

A shirtless man in black pants stood busily scrubbing his face.

"You the local law?" McCoy asked.

The man dried, flung the towel onto the table near the basin and nodded. "Yep. Can't you see the silver star pinned on my chest?"

Spur nodded.

The man slipped on a gray muslin shirt. "Name's Frank. Tex Frank. And before you ask me what I'm doing with a name like Tex in the middle of Kansas, it's short for my real name, Tezcatlipoca." Frank tucked in the tails. "And before you ask me what in hell that means, my father was interested in Mexican shit and he slapped that moniker on me. So you don't have to ask me why I like to be called Tex." Done dressing, the man smoothed down the shirt and smiled. "So what can I do for you?"

Blinking at the man's unusual verbal style, McCoy stuck out his hand. "I'm Spur McCoy."

"Don't ask me to shake your hand," Tex said. But he laughed and quickly pumped it.

"Right. I'm here in town looking for someone."

Frank sighed. "If you can't find her in one of our saloons, you just ain't looking."

"No, a man. He went by the name of Joshua Golden in Holmes but his real name seems to be Jack T. Galde."

Tex sat behind his chair and started shuffling a deck of cards. "Hmmm. Nope. Doesn't sound familiar." He rippled the deck. "You a sheriff, too?"

"Sure. See the star on my chest?"

Frank guffawed. "Point taken."

"No, I'm with the government. Secret Service."

A whistle. "Well, I sure as shit've heard about you folks but never expected to meet one of you."

Shuffle. Shuffle.

He peered at Spur with a cocked head. "How do I know you just ain't farting out hot air about this?"

"I've got papers proving my identity back in my hotel room and can bring them to you."

Cards slapped against each other, interlacing, merging into a single stack, only to be divided once again by bony fingers. "No, no. I pride myself on being a good judge of character. You seem to be who you say you are. So why're you looking for this—who the hell was it?"

The man's manner and his constant card-play were annoying but this was his only possible source of information in the town. "Galde. Jack T. Galde. I'm convinced that he's the man who's been robbing small towns all over this part of Kansas, in a line stretching west from Kansas City. He's hit five banks so far and killed at least twelve men and women."

The shuffling halted momentarily, then continued. "Sounds like a real bastard." Tex's face went dark. "You think he's here in Fagan?"

Spur nodded. "Friend of mine saw him just yesterday in the Red Ace Saloon. And he may be registered at the Jason Lomax Inn under the name of Jake Gould."

He sighed. "Trying to find him in this crowd'd be harder than finding a virgin in the Four Jacks." He rippled the cards again, shuffling, shuffling.

"I don't know for sure, but I think he tried to kill my friend—a lady—last night in her room in the Crouching Lion Hotel."

"Ah. Patrice Carlon. I heard about that. Seems she set fire to her room, burned up a rug, a table and some curtains, then disappeared."

Spur grinned. "I was there when it happened. Someone shot through her window and knocked over a lamp. That's what started the fire. And as for her disappearing she spent the night in my room."

The sheriff nodded. "Well, I don't know what to tell you. If this Galde is in town to rob my bank I sure as hell'd like to get him. And even if he ain't thinking to do any thievery, a man like that—a woman killer—don't deserve to enjoy his breath." He slapped the cards down onto the table and rose. "Anything I can do to help you, you just let me know."

"I sure will, Sheriff Frank. I don't know that you can help me; just wanted to warn you of possible future troubles in this little town of yours."

"Yeah. Never hurts." Tex's face was a mask of boredom but tinged with intrigue.

"You—you got something about those cards?"

Tex smiled. "Keeps me from drinking."

McCoy shook the man's hand and walked out of the office. Before he closed the door behind him he once again heard the shuffle, shuffle, shuffle of the devil's picture book.

11

After grabbing lunch with Patrice, who said she
was still sleepy from last night's exertion and
wanted to take a nap, McCoy left her in his room
and walked the streets of Fagan, searching for Jack
T. Galde. As he assumed, however, there were far
too many people in the town, far too many faces to
watch.

Taking a new approach, Spur went to the small,
white church that sat a hundred yards out of town.
Inside the air was still, dusty and heated by the
relentless sun. At first he figured that it was empty
but a grunt from between the first two rows of
pews told him he was wrong. Spur walked up the
middle aisle to find a man dressed in black,
crouched down on his knees and reaching under
the front pew.

"Preacher?" he said.

Startled by the voice, the man banged his head

on the wood seat, said something low and unintelligible and slowly rose to his feet. As soon as his face was visible McCoy relaxed. It wasn't Galde.

"Hello!" the wrinkled preacher said, rubbing the red circle of bare flesh that surmounted his skull. "I'm afraid you took me by surprise. That wasn't the most dignified position for you to catch me in. Sorry about that," the round-eyed, sweet-faced old man said.

"No problem. I didn't think you were here."

The wizened man waved around with both hands. "I'm always here. Morning, noon and night. I even sleep in a little room off from the altar, just to be sure that whenever one of my flock needs help I'm there. What can I do for you?"

"Well, it's kind of hard to explain. Have any preachers come here recently from out of town, looking for work, or to start up a new church?"

The man shook his head. "No. Thankfully, no. Some of my flock seem to think I'm too old to keep on doing this. If any new man had shown up I'd suppose I'd be sitting somewhere doing nothing, reading the Bible and rotting." He dusted off his large hands.

Spur nodded. "I didn't think so. Actually, the man I'm looking for isn't really a preacher but a bankrobbing murderer by name of Jack T. Galde, or Joshua Golden."

"May God forgive him of his sins," the elderly man automatically said. "You believe this—ah, gentleman has recently arrived here in Fagan?" He scratched his left leg.

"I know he has. He was seen a few days ago.

Since Galde used a preacher's disguise in the last town he was in, I thought that he might have—"

The old man smiled. "I see. Well, I hope you don't think I'm this Galde. That is, unless he was sixty years old, bald and truly devoted to our Lord."

Spur held up his hands. "No, sir. I don't believe you're him. But if any new preachers come in to see you, let me know, okay? I'm staying at the National Hotel. Name's Spur McCoy."

"Fine. I'll do that. Well, I've got to retrieve that hymn book. It's somewhere down there under that pew." He hesitated and stared meaningfully at it.

Spur grunted, bent down and picked up the book. "Here you go, preacher. And thanks."

The man beamed. "Thank you, Mr. McCoy. Good day."

Galde sat in a corner of Smith's Saloon, nursing the bottle he'd bought two hours earlier. He set the half-empty whiskey on the table, burped, shoved the unruly black hair from his eyes and frowned.

He had to kill her, he knew. Had to silence the little bitch. But how? He couldn't rush into the Red Ace Saloon and blast her head off while she was dancing. Too risky and he'd just get himself killed.

Though he'd always worked alone, Galde found himself considering hiring on some extra guns. Always prideful of the excellent work he'd done up to this point the thought of using other men didn't appeal to him. But this was a crisis situation, one that he had to take care of immediately if he wanted to save his ass from the gallows.

He slumped lower in his chair and took another swallow from the bottle. As always the alcohol soothed him even as it burned up his guts.

Okay. Tonight. That'd be as late as he could move. He'd get the girl tonight, take her out of town and kill her. The old feelings stirred in him: the excitement of the chase, the thrill of seeing bright blood spattered onto the ground, the ecstasy of determining who lived and who died.

Two young men walked by, sucking whiskey, packing six-guns. They looked like the type of men he needed—old enough to have experience but young enough not to give a damn about what they did.

"Hey, come over here!" Galde said.

The taller, slimmer of the two glanced at him and snarled. "Leave us the fuck alone, fat man!" he said, and guzzled another mouthful.

"Yeah! We're gonna go screw some women!" His shorter friend grabbed his crotch and lewdly squeezed it.

Galde controlled his temper. "Fine. Then you *boys* go find your girls. Guess I was wrong. Guess you wouldn't be interested in earning fifty-dollars tonight." He looked away from them.

Four feet scrambled over to his table. The flushed, drunken youths stared at him.

"What'd you say? Fifty-dollars?" The older one said, quickly losing his snarl.

Galde smirked. Always gets them by the balls—money that is. "No, go on and get your women if you don't have time to talk to me."

The two sat at his table. "Hey, mister, anything you want done we can do. Ain't that right, Kurt?"

he said, slamming down his bottle.

"Yeah, Matt. Whadya want us to do?"

Galde smoothed on a smile. "You boys old enough to work for me?"

"Shit, I'm twenty, and Matt here's nineteen," Kurt said, his bloodshot eyes focusing on the pudgy man. "That's old enough for anything you could have in mind." He burped. Twice.

Galde had already decided to try them out. He had a gut feeling about the pair, a talent he'd honed on the rough streets of New York.

He let them sweat it out for a few minutes, glancing at one, the other, then away, drumming his fingers on the slick, ash-covered table.

"Come on, mister, what do we gotta do to get that money?" Matt asked.

"Can you boys keep your big mouths shut? Can you do what I tell you to do, take the money and get the hell out of town for a few days?"

"Shore!" Kurt said.

"Shit; with money like that I'd kiss this town's ass goodbye and ride outa here faster than you could spit!"

Galde snorted. "If you're still interested tonight, show up behind the livery stable at dusk. Don't bring anyone with you and don't tell anyone you're going there. I'll let you in on everything you need to know then. Now get your butts off those chairs and leave me alone."

The two youths stood, nodded, flushed, swallowed more whiskey and wandered away.

Galde watched them go. They'd be there, eager. They'd do anything he wanted to get their hands on that kind of money. And after they'd helped him

get the big-mouthed bitch he might even pay them.
He patted the revolver in his holster.

Might.

"Nervous?" Spur asked Patrice as they entered
the Red Ace Saloon.

She looked at him and pulled a lock of blonde
hair from her forehead. "About dancing? No. I'm
used to it by now. But I'm sure not too happy
thinking that that man might come in here again
tonight." She blew out her breath and shook her
head. "Why don't we leave? Tonight? Let's go back
to Holmes. You can ride me there and I'll get the
next train back home. I'm tired of this place, tired
of the men and—"

Spur smiled. "It'd be more dangerous for you to
ride at night than it would be to dance up there in
those lights." He stroked her arm. "Relax, Patrice.
If you still feel that way tomorrow morning I'd be
glad to accompany you back to Holmes. Or, at least
see you off at the train if it comes through here. Try
to put it out of your mind."

Patrice's pretty face fell. "That's easy for you to
say. You don't have a crazy fake preacher trying to
kill you."

"Now don't think about it. Just dance up a storm
out there. If you are going back home tomorrow
you might as well do it with a little extra money."

"You're right, of course." She clasped his hand,
blew him a kiss and disappeared backstage.

Spur got a drink and settled in at a small table at
the rear of the saloon. It quickly filled with noisy,
armed men eager for a little diversion from their
daily lives. Spur took it all in, checking every face,

looking for harsh features and black hair attached to a fat, short body.

Galde didn't show up.

He smiled curtly as two youths settled in at his table.

"Sorry, mister," the younger said as he sat down, "last table in the place."

He waved his lack of concern and nursed on his whiskey. After seeing Patrice safely through the show and then into his bed he'd check room 305 of the Jason Lomax Inn. Maybe this Jake Gould was Jack Galde, maybe not. But it was high time he found out.

The six dancers came on stage in tight silk dresses, all red, all designed to show off every curve of their bodies. The men watching them hooted and hollered, slamming their boots onto the wooden floor and nudging each other as they shouted what they'd do to the girls.

Patrice shined as she moved through the first dance, an uncomplicated romp across the stage. The two men seated on either side of Spur stared at the women unblinkingly, drinking whiskey, panting.

"Hell, Kurt, have you *ever* seen such fine female flesh?" one slurred.

"Fuck, no. Not out there on the ranch. Sure puts me in mind of doing something but just lookin' at them." He stumbled to his feet.

Kurt grabbed the back of his pants and yanked his friend down onto his chair. "Just sit there, Matt. Don't forget we gotta work tonight."

"Aw hell! Fuck the money!"

Kurt leaned across Spur. "Now you listen here,

boy! We're gonna do our work and collect our pay.
We're a team. If you run off, leaving me alone, I
won't get a goddamned dime! Just watch the
fuckin' show!''

Spur leaned away from the streams of sodden
breath that the youth shot across his face. Boys will
be boys, he thought.

''Oh—oh, hell. Okay, Kurt. I guess'll it be worth
it.'' He grumbled into his drink.

McCoy sighed and watched as Patrice went
through the dazzling moves. The piano player was
far better than the one who'd provided the music at
her former place of employment, but his efforts
were nearly drowned out by the hoots and
thundering, full-throated yells that the overexcited
men blasted out at the women.

The number ended and the women bowed, then
quickly began the second. As they leapt and
kicked, showing off their finely-shaped legs and
petticoats, a beefy, red-faced man stood and
walked toward the stage.

Spur was instantly behind him. From the back
the man could be Galde, though he hadn't seen the
thief enter the saloon. He tapped him on his back.

''Leave me the fuck alone!''

Spur grabbed his shoulders and spun him
around. It was Enoch Salt, the father who'd
threatened to kill that boy for taking his daughter
on a walk.

The whiskey-lubricated man glared at McCoy,
rocking back and forth on unsteady feet. ''Hell, I'm
first!'' he yelled. ''You can have 'em later.'' He

struggled against Spur's powerful grip. "Let me go, dammit!"

"Sit down, Salt! Those are dancing girls, not whores! No one's having them—any of them."

"The hell I ain't!" he said. "Just try to stop me! I'm gonna fuck 'em right on the goddamned stage!"

Spur released the man and slammed his doubled-up fist into Salt's jaw. The blow didn't faze the man.

He grinned. "You tryin' to pick a fight with me?" His hand flew down to his holster.

Spur blocked Salt's grab and jerked the arm backward into an unnatural position. Enoch howled as McCoy punched him in the gut, driving his fists into the fleshy belly, forcing him backward with the force of his blows.

Salt banged against a table, upsetting it and spilling him to the ground. A whiskey bottle smashed beside him as cards and poker chips rained down on the big man. He groaned, lifted his head, then slumped, unconscious.

The music halted. Patrice and the other girls on stage stood looking at the downed man.

"Er, go ahead with the show, ladies," McCoy said, and tipped his hat at Patrice.

She smiled. As the dancers started kicking away Spur dragged the big man over to his table, huffed and sat in his chair. The man was heavy.

"Mighty fancy fist work," Matt said, grinning.

"Thanks." Crossing his legs, he rested his heels on Enoch Salt's stomach and watched the rest of the show.

By the time it was over Salt still hadn't moved.

Spur bent toward him and felt the man's wrist. He was alive but still unconscious. He poured his drink onto the man's face.

"Come on, wake up!" he said.

Salt spluttered, blubbered, and wiped the stinging liquid from his eyes. "What—wh—"

"On your feet, man. You've got a date with the sheriff."

With tremendous effort he lifted the huge man, draped his left arm around his shoulder and dragged him from the saloon. Patrice emerged from backstage as McCoy neared the door.

"Hey! Where you going, Spur?" she called.

"Sheriff's. I'll be right back." He turned and threw her his room key. "Go there and stay inside. Don't open the door for anyone but me, Patrice. I'll be back soon as I have this lover locked up for the night."

Groaning, he dragged him off to the sheriff's office four blocks away.

Patrice fanned her face. She was tired, as always, after her energetic performance. All through the hour-long show the blonde had looked forward to its conclusion and to once again sharing Spur's room. The hungry-eyed men in the saloon disturbed her, but the pleasing absence of Galde made it tolerable. She refused a dozen offers of drinks from a variety of men and sat sipping her ginger ale at the table closest to the bar, where she felt safe.

Tired, scared, she tried to rouse enough energy and courage within her to walk to Spur's hotel. It wasn't far but, it was far enough to make her hesitate. Why the heck did he have to go and leave her alone like that?

Two young men approached her. Patrice sighed, readying her response of "No, thank you; I'm drinking sarsaparilla."

"Ma'am," one of the youths said, and pulled his hat from his head. "Me and Matt here was wonderin' if you'd allow us the honor of escorting you to your hotel."

Well, at least the boys were trying a new approach. "I'm sorry, but I'm waiting for my friend—the one that beat up the big, strong man a few minutes ago?" She fluttered her eyelashes and turned away from them.

"But—but—"

"No thank you." Her words were even, level, tinged with the slightest bit of anger.

"Look, ma'am, we just want to—"

"These two boys bothering you, Patrice?"

She turned. Elias Weatherby walked up to her table, glaring at them behind thick, round glasses.

"They were just leaving, boss."

"Fine. Get the hell outa my saloon! If I catch you bothering one of my girls again I'll do more than kick you out!"

"You don't scare us!"

"Come on, Matt, let's go! We have to talk!" He slurred his words.

Kurt dragged his friend out of the bar.

Patrice sighed. "Thanks, Mr. Weatherby."

The middle-aged man smiled paternally at her. "No problem. Always like to look after my girls. You have someone to walk you home?"

"No," she said. "He had to take that man to the

sheriff's office."

"Allow me."

Pleased, Patrice rose and the two left the saloon. Outside the air was cool, refreshing. She felt safe with him, safer than she would have walking alone or even with one of the questionable men from the saloon. They walked along, arm in arm, through alternating patches of light and darkness as they passed the kerosene street lamps that dotted the broad avenue.

Patrice was wrapped up in her thoughts. Should she tell Mr. Weatherby that she was leaving in the morning? It wouldn't be right not to. But why mess up things before she absolutely had to? But then again. . . .

They passed another light. A dark alley yawned near them. Patrice turned to him. "Mr. Weatherby, I have to talk to you about something."

He gestured with his right hand. "Talk away. I already think of you as my daughter, Patrice."

"Well, it's about my job."

"You don't like working for me?"

"No. Not that at all. It's just that I don't know how much longer I can stay here in Fagan. There's this man—"

Powerful hands gripped her waist, twisting her from the man's arm. Patrice screamed as a shadowy figure slammed the butt end of a revolver onto her employer's head. He slumped to the ground.

A hand quickly covered her mouth, muffling her shrieks. She kicked, flailed her arms and bit at the grasping fingers as the two men pulled her into the bowels of the alley.

12

The man's weight around his arm felt like it was about to snap his knees. Groaning, Spur yanked, pulled and shoved a blubbering Enoch Salt toward Sheriff Tex Frank's office.

Salt drowsed along the way, his big body slumping down, further hindering their progress. Each time the man's chin hit his chest McCoy backhanded him, rousing Salt for another half-block or so.

It took him nearly ten minutes to clear the distance between the Red Ace Saloon and the sheriff's office. He finally halted before the closed door, yanked the knob and kicked it open.

He shoved Enoch Salt forward. The big man stumbled, blinked at the bright light and melted into a heap of pulsing flesh at Tex Frank's feet.

"Brought you some company," Spur said.

"I can see that. What's old Salt done now? Tried

to kill Tommy again? Or maybe looked up old Gussie Graysom's dress?'' The sheriff chuckled.

''He tried to rape six ladies in full view of thirty or so men.''

Tex whistled. ''Red Eye Saloon, right? That's the first time he's tried that—at least in that saloon.''

''He's drunker than a skunk. I tried to stop him but he wouldn't quit so I punched him.'' Spur rubbed his knuckles. ''When that didn't make a dent I pounded his gut for a couple minutes. He finally crashed into a table and went out like a lamp on a windy day.''

''I'll look after him. You—you brought him here all by yourself?''

''Sure. Why?''

''Oh, nothing. It's just that Salt must weight three-hundred pounds.''

McCoy shrugged. ''Need me for anything else? I have a lady waiting for me.''

''Nope. Thanks.'' The sheriff walked to his desk and reached for the well-thumbed paying cards.

They slapped against the polished wood as Spur left to go find Patrice—safely locked in his room, he hoped.

Suffocating, she bit. Salty blood flooded into her mouth as Patrice sunk her teeth into the tender fingers, ripping them, tearing flesh from bone.

''Shit!'' the shadowed man whispered as he hustled her down the dark alley. He slapped her cheek. ''Fuckin' bitch like to tore off my finger!''

She coughed, spat blood, gagged against the relentless, pressure.

''Grab her throat but keep her quiet!'' Kurt said

as they neared the alley's rear.

Hands tightened beneath her chin. Patrice gasped, gagged as her air was cut off. Frightened and enraged, she drove her knee into her captor's groin. He screamed and dropped to the ground, freeing her head.

"What the fuck—"

Patrice elbowed the second man, taking him by surprise. Butting his chest with her blonde head the woman succeeded in shoving him back against the wall.

"Hell!" he said.

She jabbed her foot between the man's legs as he went for her. For one terrifying second he gripped her foot, threatened to tear off her leg, then sank to the ground with a groan.

"Don't let her get away!"

Jubilant, Patrice shot down the alley, her skirt rustling and dragging in the dirt. She wiped the slimy vein juice from her lips and forced her legs as fast as they'd go.

Sooner than she'd hoped, she heard the men following behind her. Where to go? Her mind raced as she exited the alley, not stopping to glance down at her prone employer. Without thinking she turned to the right and ran for the saloon.

If only it was still open—Light spilled from below its doors half a block down.

"Fuck Galde. I'm gonna kill her myself! She smashed my balls something fierce!"

Fast. Faster. Patrice felt her legs ache, her heart protesting at the unprecedented strain that she was forcing it into.

"Get her! *Kill her*!"

Panting, sickened from the taste of blood, Patrice raced into the Red Ace Saloon.

"Jule! Your gun!" she gasped, her legs faltering as she tried to clear the floor between the door and the man. "They're—tried to kill—coming now!"

The piano player whipped out a Colt .45 and trained it on the door. "Hang tight, Patrice!" he shouted.

Matt and Kurt stormed in, weapons drawn. Jules fired twice, shattering the ceiling over their heads. The startled men bolted from the saloon as fast as they'd entered it.

Patrice looked away long before the explosions had stopped echoing in the saloon. She squeezed her eyes shut as her ears rang from the gunshots. Revulsion rose in her throat. "Are—are they dead?"

"Nope," Jule said. "But they're gone."

She sighed.

"I don't think they're coming back, but I better get you into Mr. Weatherby's office. It's safer there." The piano player paused. "Hey, you all right, Patrice?"

"No."

She was sick all over the floor.

Spur ran back to his hotel and up the stairs. He banged on the door. "Patrice!" he yelled. "Patrice, you in there?"

No answer. The short hairs on the back of his neck itched. Either she wasn't in there or she couldn't answer.

He slammed his shoulder against the door, once, twice, hurling all his weight and strength into the

move. The second impact sent it buckling on its
hinges. It flew open.

His room was dark. Spur turned up the flame.

It was also empty.

Galde fidgeted in the darkness as he waited by
his horse a hundred yards from the livery stable.
The two boys should have been there five minutes
ago as far as he could reckon. Where the hell were
they?

This was why he didn't use help. *This* was why
he worked alone. If something went wrong he
only had himself to blame, not empty-headed
youths or trigger-happy gunmen.

Three minutes later the two youths ran up to
him, holding their crotches. They were alone.

Rage boiled in his gut. He knew they'd fail. He
knew it!

"Stop playing with your dicks and tell me where
the fuck the girl is!" he blasted.

"Jesus!" Matt said. "She—she—"

Kurt grimaced but stood tall in front of the man.
"We lost her, Galde. She got away. And damn near
took our balls with her!" He massaged his groin.

"I shoulda known better than to trust two *boys*
like you," Galde said, fuming.

"But she didn't do it alone," Matt said. "We
knocked out her boss but this other guy showed up
and shot at us."

He sneered. "So you shit your pants and came
crawling back here." He shook his head. "Damn!"

"Hey look, Galde, we tried. We did our best!"
Kurt slammed his fist into his hand.

"Right."

He turned around, pondering. What to do? What to do? His hand slid under his coat to the sheath that hung from his belt.

Which first. Which first.

After a minute, Galde turned around. "All right, boys, I guess it couldn't be helped," he said.

"Then—then you're not mad at us anymore?" Matt asked, his voice filled with astonishment.

Galde smiled at the nineteen-year-old boy. "Mad? Hell no. Anyone could have fucked that up. She's not an easy girl anyway you look at it."

In the white light spilling down from the moon above, Kurt's face relaxed. "Gee, that's awful nice of you."

"Since you tried I might as well pay you boys something for your trouble."

"You—you don't have to do that," Matt said.

"Shut *up*, Matt!" Kurt poked him in his side.

Galde grinned and approached the two young men. They stood shoulder to shoulder, close enough for a fast, clean job. "I've got my money right here in my pocket." He pretended to fumble around in his coat. "This should pay you for all the work you've done for me."

The knife flashed up and into Kurt's chest, ripping, tearing, plunging full-length. He quickly yanked it out and stabbed Matt's heart, twisted it, withdrew and sheathed it again in Kurt's gaping wound.

The young men coughed liquidly, their eyes wide, screams gurgling in their throats. Galde sliced up their chests with powerful strokes, switching from one to the other, cutting into their bodies like they were hard butter.

Bones snapped under the knife blade. Tissue ruptured. The two young men's hearts beat slower, spasmed, pumped blood out of the slits in their chests.

Matt sunk to his knees, his arms jerking as Galde plunged his knife one last time into Kurt's body and savagely ripped it out. The twenty year old youth slumped to the ground, coughed, lay still.

Trembling wth rage and exultation, Galde turned his attention to Matt. Even when the youth slammed down on his back he continued stabbing, grunting, sweating, straining as the sickly stench of fresh human blood filled his nostrils. He hacked him to death.

Finished, Galde removed his knife, threw it into the trees behind him and stood, shaking, smiling. He glanced down at the bodies, kicked them and walked to the water barrel to wash the evidence off his hands and clothes.

They wouldn't fail him again.

"Patrice!" Spur yelled as he burst into the Red Eye Saloon.

Jule met him with a gun. McCoy quickly learned what had happened from the piano player and went into Mr. Weatherby's office. He gathered the woman up in his arms and carried her to Frank Tex's office.

"Could you keep her here for awhile?" McCoy asked the surprised young sheriff.

"Sure. Always have room for a fine looking lady." Tex tipped his hat.

"She was nearly kidnapped again. At least three

men want her dead.'' Spur pointed at the man.
''Don't let me down, Frank!''

''I won't. Trust me.''

Spur headed for the door.

''Hey, McCoy! Where you going?'' Tex asked.

''To find Jack T. Galde!''

Rushing with the thrill of the murder, Galde
walked his horse down the main street, brazenly
daring any of the few men on the street to accuse
him of anything. He'd remove all traces of blood
from his clothing, hands and arms, and had left the
knife in the woods. He was safe for now but knew
he had to get out of town as fast as possible.

No sense in sneaking out, he told himself. He'd
already checked out of his room, his horse was
loaded with his money and those few possessions
he'd decided to bring with him. It was time to
leave.

Rain fell, light at first, then more heavily. With
confidence bursting through him, Galde didn't
flinch as he approached the sheriff's office.
Glancing inside, however, made him falter. He
saw a flash of blonde hair as the sheriff ushered a
woman into the jail in the rear.

Patrice Carlon? He shrugged. Might as well clean
up one last problem before he left.

After tying up his horse in front of the sheriff's
office, he walked in.

''Sheriff!'' he called. ''Anybody in there?''

''Just a minute.'' The man's voice came from the
doorway that connected the jail with the rest of the
office.

Galde went to it, pressed his back against the wall and drew. He waited, patiently.

Tex Frank walked out. "What can I do for—"

He pushed the Colt's barrel against the man's side and fired. The bullet lodged deep inside the sheriff's body. Tex groaned and groped at his holster but Galde fired again, slamming a lead slug into Frank's chest. The man dropped.

He grabbed the keyring that stuck out of the sheriff's pocket and hustled into the jail.

There were two cells. One contained a snoring drunk. In the other—

Galde tried the first key. It opened the lock. Patrice looked up at him.

"Not you! Not again!" she wailed.

He stormed to her, back-handed her into a daze, scooped her off her feet and carried her outside into the driving rain.

Galde threw the woman onto the saddle, mounted up and rode fast out of town, gripping her unconscious body with his powerful thighs as he left Fagan behind him forever.

"Jake Gould checked out three hours ago," the bored young woman behind the registry at the Jason Lomax Inn said after he'd asked.

"You sure?"

She smirked. "That's my job, mister."

Spur hurried out and walked through the rain back to Tex Frank's office. Nothing. He didn't know where Galde was, what he was doing. What the hell was happening?

His hat's broad brim drooped, sending a shower of chilling water onto his face. Spur wiped it away and hurried as the rain suddenly stopped and the moon came out from behind the clouds.

The front door lay open. He drew and cautiously advanced on the office. Walking inside, Spur sighed. Tex Frank lay in a small pool of blood. He stepped over the man and checked the jail cells. Patrice, of course, was gone.

Moving back into the office he looked down. The dead sheriff's hand lay sprawled near a dark red smear on the floor.

Galde. It must have been Galde.

He ran outside. Fresh horse tracks led away from the sheriff's office to the west. Judging from the depth of the impressions they'd been made by a horse carrying two people.

Spur ran for his mare, his boots splashing mud over his pants.

Dammit! Dammit! Dammit!

13

Patrice dreamed.

She was back in her parent's home in St. Louis.
The large brick building was comforting in its
familiarity. The scent of roses from vases placed
before the windows filled the air. Curled up in the
library in front of the fireplace on a huge couch,
was Patrice. She clutched the oversized leather
bound volume of Shakespeare in her hands,
eagerly devouring each Elizabethan word.

"Patrice, I want to talk with you."

She didn't look up. "Not now, daddy; he's just
about to meet her."

"Now!"

Something in her father's voice made her obey.
She looked up. And screamed.

Galde rose behind her father. He swung the big
axe, slicing, lopping. Her father's head rolled off
his trunk and bounced like a rubber ball across the

polished parquet floor. It stopped before her.

She dropped the book, terrified.

Her father's severed head looked up at Patrice. "You shouldn't have left home, baby! You shouldn't have left home."

Wind blasted against her cheeks. Patrice blinked, realized where she was and sighed. Rain pelted down onto her face. Cold, wet, aching, she tried to cry but the tears wouldn't come. After the terrors that she'd suffered in the last couple of days all she could do was laugh and cling to the horse's bucking neck, laugh at the absurdity of it all, laugh at what fate had dished out to her. Better to laugh than to cry.

"You finally wake up, blondie? I've been listening to your snoring for at least an hour."

Galde's voice was gruff, loud against her ear. She was immediately aware of the way his body pressed against hers, of how his arms holding the reins pinioned her sides, how his thighs molded to her legs.

"I don't snore but, yeah, Jack, I'm awake. Couldn't stay away from me, could you?"

He laughed. "No, blondie. Decided I had to throw you a fuck before I killed you. That's why I didn't slit your throat back in your cozy little cell. What were you locked up for? Whoring?"

She ignored the question and the threat. "Won't you take no for an answer?"

"I'm used to getting my way," he said into her ear.

The night was dark. Wind slashed against them, throwing up the horse's mane in rippling sprays.

The rain increased in intensity until it seemed that the sky had opened up and was pouring an ocean down on them.

Their overburdened mount strained through the sucking mud below them. It couldn't manage more than a fast walk and made its displeasure known to its rider by whinneying and snorting every few feet.

"Atta girl," Galde said to the horse. "You know, blondie, your round ass sure feels good against my dick." He pushed his rain-soaked crotch against her and rubbed up and down. "I can't wait to shove it in you."

Patrice recoiled from the contact. "You had your chance, big mouth, but you decided not to. I think I was right; you like horses. Heck, I knew you were weird the first time I saw you."

She moved forward, trying to free herself from his demanding groin, but her cramped position didn't allow her much room. Patrice was horrified to feel the man's penis erecting against her bottom, hardening, stiffening.

"Horses, huh?" Galde said. "That ain't the horse getting me ready to go like that. You'll think of horses when I'm banging you, blondie."

"Talk, talk, talk. That's all you ever do, Jack Galde!"

Maybe if she could get him to stop, she could get away. Maybe.

"Just wait, little girl. You'll get it. You'll get what you want."

Patrice sighed. "And then what? I suppose you buy me a white dress, marry me and we'll settle down on a little farm somewhere. You'll raise corn and I'll—''

He laughed. ''Go ahead, dream, blondie. I'm gonna fuck—'' he thrust his penis against her— ''fuck you to death!''

''With that little thing? Hell, you better get a couple of men to help you.'' Despite the brave words fear festered inside her, gnawing away at her courage.

''Bitch!'' He spat the word at her.

The wind howled, the rain splattered down, and the horse took them further and further from Fagan, through dim cornfields and endless acres of farmland that appeared to Patrice to comprise a gigantic, ghostly trap.

They couldn't have more than a few minutes headstart on him. Spur kicked his mare's flanks, urging the horse faster along the muddy trail. A fresh breeze blew the clouds from the sky and revealed the full moon hanging mute above him.

In the dim light he could still see the dark impressions against the duller mud beneath him. They had gone this way.

McCoy cursed as he rode, cursed at Enoch Salt, cursed at himself, but mostly cursed at Galde. The man was incredibly singleminded about Patrice Carlon. He'd kidnapped her twice, hired two men to try a third time, shot through her window and set her room on fire.

Though he was tenacious he still hadn't gotten what he wanted from the beautiful blonde-haired girl. At least he hoped he hadn't.

The trail stretched straight ahead before him, cutting a narrow path between eye-tall cornfields that looked gray in the moonlight.

Clouds swept in overhead. The light dimmed to the point where Spur could just barely make out the trail. He squinted, following the tracks, and slammed his hand down on his head as the wind threatened to whip off his hat and carry it into the air.

"Come on, girl," he said to the horse, patting its neck as the beast struggled through the mud. "They can't be far ahead. We'll get them."

The storm seemed unsure of itself, sending down showers that lasted seconds, covering and freeing the moon of its cloud cover. Ignoring the weather he rode on and on, following the dim tracks, hoping that he wasn't too late.

"Why don't you just kill me."

The words shocked Patrice even as she said them. An hour of Galde's lewd talk and the events of the last few days had broken her, leaving her an exhausted girl who was too tired to fight anymore.

"That's no way to talk, little lady," Galde said. "You gotta fight. Besides, I don't fuck dead women. That's why I never married." He guffawed.

Patrice snapped out of her mood. "Heck, no woman would ever marry you. Not unless she was deaf, dumb and blind."

"That's the spirit!" Galde chuckled. He pumped his ever-present erection against her and thrust his tongue into her wet ear.

"God! Stop it!" She squirmed, violently flinging

her head aside to free it from his mouth. The motion sent her off balance. Her body slid to the right in the saddle, pushing against Galde's arm.

"No, you don't!" he said.

She allowed him to push her up. "Fine," she said. "Well, if you're gonna do it anyway, I might as well enjoy it." She reached behind her.

"Hey, no tricks, blondie! I mean—"

Patrice slid her hand between their bodies and gripped his groin.

"I'm warning you!"

She stroked, blanking out all thoughts of what she was doing, pretending the man behind her was Spur.

"Ahhhh!"

Hating the feeling, holding back a gag, Patrice feigned interest in him. She cooed and rubbed her back against his chest as she massaged the pulsing bulge.

"Maybe I was wrong. You're not so small after all."

Only about half as big as Spur, she thought.

"That's more like it! Yeah, blondie, play with it! Play with my rod!"

They rode on.

"What're you gonna do with this thing?" she asked.

"You know!" he said, irritated. "Can't you just grope and keep your big mouth shut?"

"But I figured you'd want to keep it open. I figured you'd want me to suck you."

"Jeezus, blondie!" Galde gasped in her ear. "The way you talk I—I don't know if I—"

"Just enjoy it."

"Oh God. Stop, little lady; stop! Not yet. Jeezus!
I'm gonna—get your hands outa there!"

He halted the horse and dropped the reins. When
his arms left her sides Patrice punched his fat
crotch and slid off the horse.

"Shit!" Galde yelled.

Rain slammed down, blinding her as she landed
in the mud, rolled over and ran into the cornfield.

"Come back here, blondie! Finish what you
started! When I catch you I'll make you—"

His words were lost in the patter of raindrops on
the broad leaves and wind that rustled them.
Patrice ran blindly through the corn wincing as the
sharp bladed leaves cut her wrists and hands.
Choking with excitement and achievement, the
blonde haired woman moved deeper into the field.

It was alive with motion, as if it were the back of
a huge hairy animal. Patrice stumbled among the
stalks, darting through them without direction,
terrified that she'd hear his voice again behind her.

The storm swelled above her, dumping its load
onto the parched land. Patrice kicked off her shoes
and ran.

"There you are!"

Galde's voice terrified her.

"I see you, blondie! Guess what I have for you!
Now stand still and let me fuck you, girl!"

Patrice hyperventilated. The leaves slashed at
her soaked dress and slapped against her cheeks.
She kept on running as the crashing behind her got
louder.

"Bitch!"

Galde tackled her, his pudgy body slamming into

hers. Patrice shrieked as the stocky man drove her into the mud face first.

"Thought you could get away, huh? Not this time. You're gonna get what you want!"

Patrice pulled her head from the sucking mud and spluttered. Exhausted, she didn't resist as Galde turned her onto her back and knelt over her, straddling her legs. Patrice wiped mud from her eyes and blinked.

"All that dirty talk and your hand getting me all excited!"

Lightning crackled across the sky, outlining his bulky form. He fumbled at his crotch. "You're gonna get it."

"No. No! Not here! Not like this in the rain!" she said.

"Shut your mouth, blondie! I've waited too long."

Galde unbuttoned his pants. Though she couldn't see it she knew it hung there, ready, eager.

The thought revolted her. The thought of this man—

Patrice screamed as he threw up her soaked dress. His clammy hands gripped her thighs and spread them apart.

"Take it, bitch! You love this! You're a god-damned whore! A whore who'll do anything I want!"

She slapped at him as he ripped her petticoats off her, tore her dress to shreds. Lying there on the cold, muddy ground, huge raindrops slapping onto her nude body, Patrice Carlon screamed on and on.

"I like a bitch who fights," Galde said, as he

lowered himself onto her and the storm howled around them in the thrashing cornfield.

Wind transformed the rain drops into elemental weapons that blasted at Spur's face. Shivering, he rode his uneasy mount along the trail. Intermittent lightning terrified the horse but lit up the tracks that marked Galde's passage—horseshoe prints that were quickly melting in the rain.

A few miles out of Fagan Spur saw a dark figure on the trail ahead. He halted his horse, studied it, but couldn't make out any details. He rode slowly up to the figure and soon realized it wasn't a man.

A horse stood there next to the cornfield, water sheeting off its flanks, tossing its head. Its reins were tied to a bunch of stalks.

Galde's horse? Yes. They must have gone into the cornfield. He could have chased her in there. Spur quickly secured his mount. He wiped water from his eyes and surveyed the area. Broken stalks showed where they'd entered the field. He tore into the six-foot high sea of dripping, wind-tossed plants, following the path of destruction.

Though it didn't seem possible the storm grew stronger, the wind whipping the razor-sharp leaves around McCoy as he drove into the tall, stiff plants. The darkened sky offered him little light but Spur could just make out the trail of broken stalks before him.

The wind slapped the leaves against his body. Lightning ripped through the night, illuminating it. The trail he was following suddenly split into two paths. They'd separated. Frustrated, Spur headed down the left one.

The rain suddenly lightened but the gale force winds tugged at his body, threatening to pick him up off the ground. He bent and pushed forward as the blasting air all but obliterated the trail by flattening every single stalk of corn and then whipping them upright.

A female scream emanated from somewhere inside the field. Patrice! The scream repeated again and again. With the trail gone and wind in his ears, the cornstalks confused him. He lost his bearings and staggered around in circles between each howl before getting back on track.

Spur struggled across the field toward the voice, toward the scream, as jagged bolts of light flashed and darted above him.

14

"Hold still, blondie!" Galde said. "Dammit, let me in there, girl!"

"No. Leave me alone, Jack!" Patrice writhed beneath him, snapped her legs together and screamed. The hideous man jabbed against her stomach as he clumsily tried to penetrate the squirming woman.

Somewhere she'd found the will to fight off the evil smelling man. Patrice pressed her hands against his chest, trying to push him off her. But his wiry strength was too great for her. He grabbed her thighs and forced them open.

"Now, blondie, take it!"

Wind whipped their struggling bodies. Cornstalks broke and fell around them. Patrice slammed her legs shut again, straining them against Galde's powerful hands.

As he cursed, she grabbed one of the thick stalks

from his back. *Use it,* she told herself. *Use it to stop him.*

Patrice slammed its blunt end down against his back.

"What the—" he said.

She smacked it onto his head savagely, fighting with every ounce of strength left within her. Patrice screamed and kept flailing away with the thick stalk.

"Fucking bitch!" Galde wrestled the stalk from her hand and threw it above him where the wind carried it away. "Don't do that again!" he said, still leaning over her.

She gripped a second broken stalk and slammed it into his face, thrilling to the small victory she'd won.

Galde hit her, slapping his palm against Patrice's cheek. She ignored the pain and continued beating.

He yelled again but his words were lost to the violence of the wind that steadily increased above and around them.

Scratched, gasping, tripping over loose, wet cornstalks, Spur ran toward the screams. She should be straight ahead, but by the way the wind shifted and moved around him like a conscious being, he knew that he could be hurrying toward the wrong spot while Galde . . . .

It had been a long time since he'd witnessed a midwestern storm and he'd forgotten how powerful they could be. Flashes of blueish white light sparkled continually in the puddles before him as he struggled to save Patrice.

There, in the distance, in a blinding flash of lightning, he saw two figures on the ground ahead of him. A man and a woman. Patrice. Patrice and Jack Galde.

McCoy drew his Colt .45 as he approached the struggling pair. He was raping her. The bastard was raping her!

"Galde!" he yelled, but the words drifted above him. A hundred feet separated them. Spur ran as the air filled with leaves and stalks and dirt clods that swirled and eddied and danced.

A mass of airborne earth splattered against his face. He cursed and wiped his face, hurrying toward the pair.

Fifty feet.

"Galde!" he howled. "Leave her the fuck alone!"

He still couldn't hear him but from the way the man and woman wrestled it was clear that he hadn't raped her yet. He'd arrived just in time.

Spur fired a shot into the air and bounded toward them. Even when he got into range he still couldn't get a clean shot that wouldn't hit Patrice as well.

"Dammit, Galde!"

He was twenty feet away.

The shadowed man whipped around to face Spur, gripping a naked Patrice to his chest.

"Go ahead and shoot, fucker! Go ahead!" Galde screamed. "Shoot, but you'll have to kill your little bitch if you want to kill me!"

More lightning. McCoy had to lean forward to prevent the slamming wind from throwing him onto his back. "Come on, Galde. It's over. Let the girl go."

The big man laughed. "Fuck you!"

"You can't escape this time. There's no way out."

"Throw down your gun! Throw it behind you and let me and blondie here go. Do that and I won't kill you!" he shouted above the wind. Still pinning Patrice to his chest, Galde drew his revolver and pressed it against the woman's head. "You got that, mister? Throw it down or she dies!" he screamed.

Spur hesitated. "If you kill her then I won't have any reason not to kill you."

"Hah! You won't take the chance. I got all the cards, mister. Drop your weapon and back off!"

McCoy started to respond, then looked above the dimly lit man. Lightning lit up a huge funnel cloud that twisted and moved across the flat land, eating it up in its elemental hunger, whirling the earth into a chaotic ruin. It moved straight toward them.

Spur stalled. "Hell, Galde," he said, glancing at the tornado. "Maybe you're right."

The fat man laughed. "Course I'm right. I'm always right. Now throw down your gun."

In less than a minute the tornado would be close if not directly overhead. He raised his arm over his head, as if to fling his Colt behind his head.

"Well! What're you waiting for?" Galde screamed.

Spur stared at him.

The wind intensified, blasting their bodies, whipping the broken cornstalks into tortured flight.

"What the hell?" Galde yelled.

"Bad storm!"

The man slowly rose, bringing Patrice with him. He stared around at the thousands of plants that flew through the air and battered into them.

The storm's voice shrieked as it thundered down onto them. Five seconds, Spur thought, staring at Patrice's dark form.

Four. Three. Two.

One!

A tremendous wind blasted into them. Spur felt the world shake as the tornado knocked him to the ground, flattening him like it had the corn, sending him crashing to his back. His revolver flew out of his hand. The storm tugged on him, trying to rip his prone body from the earth, trying to suck his 200 pounds up into its vortex of destructive fury.

The howl was unending, eerie. Spur gripped the muddy dirt, digging his fingertips into it as he struggled to save his life. The wind tugged on his skin, pulling his face with invisible fingers until Spur felt it would rip it off.

Foot-square chunks of earth rushed up around him and disappeared into the blackness above. The ground heaved as the storm passed.

He cursed into the mud as he clung to it, riding out the tornado, hoping that it would spare Patrice but take Galde into its spout.

Finally it lessened, grew weaker. McCoy searched for his revolver, patting the ground beside him with his hand even as the tornado still pressed against his chest. It wasn't there.

Damn! He heard Patrice's screams above the wind as he struggled against it, raising his torso with tremendous effort, gasping for breath.

Lightning crackled overhead. He glanced over. The two still laid side by side on the ground as Spur searched for his gun. A renewed blast of air sent him crashing onto his back, knocking the oxygen from his lungs. Moaning, he lay there, still fumbling for his weapon. Where the hell had it gone?

Finally, he scrambled onto his knees and dove into a four-foot high mound of cornstalks next to him. The gun, he told himself. Get the gun. Forget everything else and get the goddamned gun!

McCoy slid through the sharp leaves and thick stalks, pushing through them, frantically searching. He dug to the bottom of the pile. Nothing. Damn!

He poked his head out from the vegetation. Patrice lay sobbing where she'd been while Galde was on his hands and knees, throwing leaves over his shoulder.

Good. He didn't have his gun either. Spur lunged into another, larger pile and searched it. As he did so the storm suddenly dropped off. The silence was incredible.

"I'll kill you!" Galde said.

"You gotta find your gun first! Why don't you get on your horse and get the hell outa here!" Spur said.

"No way! I don't leave jobs half-done!"

Where the fuck was it? He burrowed into the pile, grasping, digging, looking, spitting shredded leaves from his lips and pushing them from his eyes.

Something hard pressed against his hand. He gripped the stock and shot to his feet only to see Galde's back disappearing into the darkness. He fired over his shoulder.

Damn!

Patrice lay curled up on the ground, naked, crying.

As the tornado's eye passed overhead the eerie calm was shattered by deadly winds. Spur fought them, walking into its force. It shut his eyes, pounded at his legs. Like a blind man, he stumbled forward toward the departing Galde. He kicked and ran even as the storm pushed the air out of his lungs and left him gasping. Get him, he told himself. Get him!

It soon lessened. Cursing, he peeled open one eye and looked down at Patrice who lay at his feet.

"You okay?" he shouted.

She shivered and clutched her arms to her bare breasts, but nodded.

"I'll be back!"

The tornado had cleared a path though the corn-field, stripping it clean. Spur ran through it toward the horse that he hoped would still be waiting for him. The wind kicked up globules of mud as he raced through it, fighting for breath.

It was impossible to see where Galde was but he ran on, hoping he'd hit the trail somewhere near his horse.

Finally he was there. His horse stood ten feet away—alone. He twisted around his head, searching the trail in both directions, but saw nothing but blackness.

Damn!

He couldn't leave Patrice there.

The cursing man ran back through the stripped cornfield and quickly squatted beside her. The wind had died to a stiff breeze.

"Patrice," Spur said. He shucked off his coat as the naked woman sat up on the ground. "Here. Wear this."

Patrice slipped it around her shoulders. "I just wanted to say—thanks." Her voice was thin.

He nodded, scooped her up in his arms and stood. He carried Patrice back to his horse.

"He got away," she said, shivering and pulling the coat tighter around her.

"For now. I'll get him. Don't you worry your pretty little head about that."

She nodded. "If you hadn't gotten here just then, he would have—he would have raped me."

"I know."

She looked up at the man who carried her. "Who are you, Spur McCoy?" The battered woman's voice was charged with wonder. "Who the hell *are* you?"

"It's a long story. We'll talk about it later. Now I have to get you back to town."

She gripped his arm. "No. I mean NO! Let's get him first. I can wait here, or ride with you." She laughed. "Heck, I'm used to that."

"Okay."

They made it to his horse. The beast stamped, flung its head back and forth as the tornado finally left the area. Rain splashed down onto them as Spur deposited Patrice on his saddle. He slipped up behind her and kicked the mare's flanks.

The excited, frightened beast bolted into action. Figuring that Galde wouldn't return to Fagan, he rode west into the steadily increasing rain.

Patrice reached down and gripped her legs.

"Why—why would that man do this to me?"

"I don't know, Patrice." He kissed the top of her head as they rode.

The sky opened up, pouring down huge drops. The ground quickly turned into a liquid mass of thick mud. The horse faltered, whickered and slowed to a walk.

Galde had a headstart. The rain was getting worse. He could feel the half naked woman shiver —uncomplainingly—in front of him.

Sighing, he turned the horse around and headed for Fagan.

"Why're you doing that?" Patrice asked.

"I just thought better of it. Plenty of time for me to catch up with him in the morning. Besides, I don't think blue skin goes so great with blonde hair."

She sighed and they rode back to town.

He cut across farmland once they approached Fagan. His newest problem: how to get her into his room in her condition without being seen. Spur finally halted his horse in a small stand of trees behind his hotel. A long stairway led up behind the building to the second floor. They should be able to make it.

But first . . . .

McCoy unbuttoned his soping wet pants and dropped them to his ankles.

"Hey, Spur," Patrice said, watching him. "We're soaking wet and I'm kinda tired."

Grunting, he pulled them over his boots and handed them to her. "Put them on. Helluva lot better for me to walk in there in my long underwear than you to be—like that." He motioned to her body.

She nodded and dressed. They dashed to the hotel, ran up the stairs and entered the hallway. A fashionably dressed, red-haired woman looked up from the key she was trying to use on her door. She blanched at the sight of the dripping, bizarely dressed people.

"Hello, Anne," Patrice said, as they shivered and hurried into his room under the woman's now amused but curious eyes.

Inside, Spur turned up the lamp, stuffed himself into dry pants and hurried out to hitch his horse in front of the hotel.

On his return Patrice was rubbing her nude body with a soft towel.

He took quickly stripped. They dried each other and jumped into bed. They struggled to get warm as they huddled under the covers. Once she'd stopped shaking from the cold Patrice turned to him, her blue eyes darting back and forth.

"Did all that really happen? I mean, I'm not dreaming, am I?"

"Afraid not. I guess you're just one unlucky woman, Patrice."

"Oh no." She shook her head. "If I was, I wouldn't have met you and I'd be—well, I don't know what I'd be now." She grabbed his hand under the quilts. "You said you'd tell me what you're doing out here. Remember?"

He nodded. "As I said, it's a long story."

She snuggled against him. "I've got all night."

As he talked Spur thought of the man who was out there, still free, riding away into another town, another disguise.

15

The storm had passed.

Exhausted, Jack T. Galde slumped in his saddle and dropped the reins. The horse nickered as she felt the man's control over her relax. Roused from his brief nap, Galde shook his head and looked around him.

Dawn broke fully, charging the eastern sky with brilliant light and stinging his eyes. Blinking, Galde yawned and surveyed his surroundings. Where the hell was he?

The land around him spread out in unvarying monotony. He'd left the farms far behind; only cresting streams, gulleys and clumps of trees broke up the landscape.

The muddy trail stretched out below him so he knew he was still headed in the right direction. During the worst of the rain he'd ridden blindly, hoping he was following the trail, hoping the tornado hadn't blown him far off course.

I feel like shit, Galde thought. Memories of last night's misadventures rocketed through his brain—the girl grabbing his crotch while they rode, running through the cornfields, trying to rape her, the tornado, the other man showing up and his hurried flight from the area.

Shame burned his cheeks. Galde punched his thigh and cursed. He *was* losing it, losing the killer instinct and the razor nerves he'd enjoyed on the dirty streets of New York. All this play acting, the waiting, the easy living, were eating him up like a worm in a corpse.

Okay, he thought. Enough of this. He was tired of the wide open spaces, tired of small town people with smaller bank accounts, tired of running, and especially tired of a certain blonde-haired bitch who was spending most of her time screwing up his life.

He added up his money in his head. Must have at least ten thousand. Hell, that's plenty. He'd head back to New York and set himself up there again. Maybe he'd open a whorehouse and charge five bucks a fuck.

Galde smiled at the idea. That'd be great. Easy living and easy robbing. Heck, it'd almost be legal stealing. It would certainly be better than what he'd been doing. Anything was better than this.

He headed back into the sunrise for Fagan. If that asshole who'd stopped him last time showed up he could take him with no problem—especially since it was daylight and there wasn't a damned tornado chewing on his butt.

Galde rode, letting the horse pick its way slowly through the four-inch deep mud, drowsing to the low sucking sounds of four hooves pushing in and out of the thick earth.

A half-hour later he saw a town in the distance. He must've passed it in the night without even seeing it. He rode on, pushing the horse harder. Maybe he could get a few hours sleep before catching the train to Kansas City.

As he approached it, however, he was quickly aware that the town was dead. Doors banged open and shut in the light breeze. Whole buildings had shifted, bent, leaned at unnatural angles. Some lay in heaps of broken wood on the ground. Weeds grew thickly through the main street. Nearby, a windmill in front of an abandoned farmhouse creaked erratically with two missing vanes.

Just my luck, Galde thought as he rode into the ghost town. The dead buildings depressed him, reminded him of how his career had been going. He snapped out of it. Sleep, I need sleep.

Galde rode among the remains of broken dreams, skirting shattered watering troughs and sun-warped barrel tines. After travelling its length he tuned back and finally stopped before the farmhouse. Should be good enough, Galde thought. Maybe he'd even find a bed.

After tying his horse up in the barn he walked on stiff legs into the house. He stepped back as the stench of rotten flesh rose up around him.

Gagging, holding his nose, Galde stared down at the decaying remains of some wild animal's lunch. Where the cow's skin hadn't been ripped from its bones it had shriveled into a dark brown mass, revealing putrifying green flesh beneath it.

The dead cow's stench was so revolting that he quickly backed out. He put his hands on his hips. This wasn't his lucky day, he thought, and settled for the barn. He remembered seeing dried hay there so at least he could make himself some kind of bed.

Galde walked into the shaded building. Shafts of light penetrated its roof, spilling onto the ground. Fatigue shot through him as he thought of sleep. Working slowly, he kicked the dried hay into a corner of the barn, near the stalls, and leaned back.

Just a little nap, Galde took himself. Just a few minutes and I'll ride back to Fagan.

Within seconds he was snoring away, lost in a nightmare filled sleep.

Spur left his hotel room before first light. The sleep had done him good. He felt strong, sharp, ready to go. Jack Galde, he thought, your time has come.

He was several miles out of town by the time the sun stained a few high clouds in front of him. Riding by the cornfield and seeing the tornado's path of destruction, Spur wondered what kind of man this Galde was. What drove him to do the things he did? What made him so bent on terrorizing a young woman who'd never done anything to anyone? What kind of man could kill innocent women, and pregnant women to boot.

He couldn't understand it, but that didn't bother him. All he had to do was stop the man, stop his rampaging path. Galde was a tornado on legs.

McCoy had left Patrice in his room, telling her to push a chair under the door and stay quiet until he returned. The sleepy girl had nodded and kissed him for luck before he left.

McCoy worried about her but realized the man who posed the greatest threat was somewhere ahead of him.

The muddy trail didn't show any fresh tracks. The rain had continued for some time after he'd turned back to Fagan.

He rode until mid-morning. By then clean horseshoe imprints dented the sun-drying mud. He had no way of knowing if they'd been made by Galde's horse or not, but it seemed likely. The distance between them indicated that the horse had been leisurely walking.

Spur raced his horse, watching the tracks blur beneath him. They continued on unbroken, clean, firm prints that stretched toward the west.

Two hours later he saw a ghost town beside the trail. Just when he was about to stop and give his mare a drink, another set of tracks from the opposite direction criss-crossed the first and trailed off toward the town.

He dismounted, squatted beside them and studied the prints. No doubt about it. They'd been made by the same horse. Galde must have changed his mind, turned around and stopped at the ruined town.

He peered at the seemingly deserted settlement. No one was in sight but the tracks led directly to it. The man was in there, somewhere. Spur rode into the town, following the prints.

Galde had ridden up and down the scrub-covered street, he learned, then headed away from it toward the ruins of a nearby farm.

He cautiously rode up to the gray farmhouse, dismounted and walked his horse closer. The mare fidgeted, fought his tugs. Spur covered its muzzle with a hand to halt its whickering. He didn't want Galde—or whoever was in there—to be warned of his approach.

The tracks led to the barn. Bootprints stretched between it and the farmhouse, then back again. Galde was in the barn.

Spur tied up his horse to a dead sapling and studied the building. It was a huge barn and looked sturdy enough. Faded red paint peeled off it like diluted, dried blood.

He walked silently, peering into the opened double-doors. All he could see were stacks of yellowed hay and patches of sunlight.

Moving with Indian silence he stopped beside the doors and listened. Above the sighing of the wind that whistled through loose timbers he heard a long, sonorous sound of snoring.

Galde was asleep.

McCoy smiled and drew his revolver. He'd reloaded it back in his hotel room. He gripped his Colt and stepped softly before the doors.

Jack Galde lay sprawled on a stack of hay. His fat belly and chest rose and fell with the rhythm of sleep. Nearby a horse stood calmly munching the dried grass.

Easy target, he thought. Almost too easy. Spur was disturbed—this wasn't like the man. Knowing something of Galde's abilities he stepped back out of the doors and moved around to the side of the barn. McCoy pressed his eye to a knothole and peered inside.

Galde continued to snore for two minutes. He suddenly sat up, fully awake, revealing the gun he'd hidden in the hay. The pudgy murderer killed off the words he'd readied on his lips and looked curiously around the barn.

Spur smiled. He'd outfoxed him. That gave him more time to decide how to approach him.

Of course it would be easy enough to simply blast the life of the man through the cracks in the wall, to be done with the man forever. But that wasn't his style or the style of the Secret Service.

Bring him alive, the directives stated. If you can't, just bring him back any way you can and have a damn good explanation of why the suspect is dead.

Galde glanced around the barn, shrugged and stood.

Spur decided it was time to move. He slipped along the wall toward the doors.

"Galde!" he yelled.

Silence.

"Galde! It's all over. Come on out!"

No answer.

Spur bent around the corner and looked inside. The horse was still there but Galde was nowhere in sight.

Where the hell had the man gone? McCoy searched the place with his eyes—none of the hay-mounds were big enough to conceal the obese man's bulk. Aside from a few broken barrels and two pitchforks the place was empty.

Even the stalls in the rear of the barn had been crushed and lay in stacks of lumber, ruling that out.

The hay loft. Spur glanced up at it. All he could see was the front of it where the wooden ladder extended down to the floor. The rest of the loft was out of his line of sight and lost in shadows.

He was up there, of course.

"Come on, Galde; I know you're up there. Give yourself up. You'll get a fair trial."

Faint snickers issued from above the barn floor.

"Don't make it hard on yourself," McCoy said.

Silence.

"What do you expect me to do, ride away and leave you here?"

"What the fuck business is it of yours?" Galde shouted. "I never did nothing to you!"

"I'm a government agent assigned to track down the man who's pulled off a string of bank robberies and murders in this state," he said evenly. "What is it—five banks so far? And thirteen murders?"

"Yeah."

"Thirteen innocent men and women. You killed women, Galde! A pregnant woman!" Spur shouted.

"Big fucking deal. She was an ugly bitch who got in my way. I do that to people who get in my way!"

"You scare me, Galde. A woman killer who breaks into banks at night when no one's around, then sneaks out of town with your tail between your legs."

He paused. No reaction. "And you couldn't even rape Patrice. You couldn't get it hard. Just what kind of a man are you, Galde?"

"Ten times what you are!" he screamed. "Get the fuck out of this barn unless you're ready to eat my lead!"

"Then come on down here and face me like a man. Stop hiding up there like a little girl. Show me your face, Galde!"

"So you can blast it off? Keep dreaming, lawman!" he snorted.

"I can wait all day." He still couldn't see a thing in the hayloft—no movement, no man.

Spur quietly moved to the ladder that led up to it and climbed. The dried wood creaked as he moved. Damn! He barged up it and fired a shot just in case the guy decided to give him a premature greeting.

"Come on up. Come on up to your death!"

Spur gripped the floor and hauled himself up. Galde stood there, weapon drawn and aimed at McCoy's chest. The fat man's face was slick with sweat but he smiled.

"You won't shoot me unless I shoot you first," he said. "Is that how you play?"

McCoy nodded. "That about sums it up." He studied the man's right shoulder, watching for movement beneath the seam-splitting gray shirt as a patch of sunlight burned into it.

"I like this kinda game."

It came. Just the faintest trembling, the tell-tale signs of muscles knotting and preparing for movement. McCoy dove as the finger squeezed. He slammed into Galde's legs, knocking him to the floor howling in rage and surprise as his bullet slammed harmlessly into the far wall.

"Jesus!" Galde yelled.

The move sent Spur's weapon skittering out of his hand. Spur grabbed the pitchfork that lay beside him and used it to flip the gun out of the man's hand. It fired as it impacted on the wooden floor ten feet away from them and skidded to the edge of the hayloft.

"Come on." He rose to his feet and towered over the thief. "Give me a good reason not to rip your guts out with this thing!" He waved the pitchfork menacingly.

The man scrambled back on his hands. "I thought you played fair," he said as his back banged against the wall.

"Not with shitheads like you!" he growled.

"W—wait! Maybe we can work something out." Galde's face crumpled with fear. "I got lots of money in my saddlebags. Take whatever you want. Just don't kill me!"

"Why shouldn't I do both?" Spur jabbed the sharp steel needles against Galde's bulging stomach.

"I got some hidden." His voice was desperate. "I'll tell you where!"

"Too late." Spur lifted the pitchfork above the cowering man, flipped it end-to-end and smashed its handle onto Galde's skull.

The man groaned and slumped over.

McCoy smiled. He should sleep for a while. The blow wasn't hard enough to have killed him, and he'd aimed for a fairly safe spot.

Just to make sure, he bent and reached for the prone man's arm with his left hand, still gripping the pitchfork.

The pulse was regular, steady.

Spur straightened up and nudged the tines against the man just to make sure he was truly unconscious. He pushed hard, harder.

Galde sprang from the wall and slid on the hay-slick floor toward his gun, a hideous scream strangling out from his throat.

He threw the pitchfork. Galde caught its business end in his hands before he slid off the hayloft and plunged, howling, ten feet down to the floor.

A scream echoed through the barn. Spur grabbed up his Colt .45 and looked over the edge, grimaced at the sight, and slowly descended the ladder.

The man and the pitchfork had changed places in the fall. It had hit the ground first, tines up. Galde had slammed into it, impaling himself on the sharp metal points.

The weight had broken off the wooden pole. Galde lay face down. Slender shafts of steel jutted out from his back.

Spur shook his head. It was over.

16

Spur lugged Galde's body onto the man's horse, tied the wrists and ankles together below its belly and led it back into Fagan. When he got there he stopped in front of the sheriff's office. He shook his head remembering that the man was dead but went in anyway.

The office was spotless. The blood stains had been scrubbed away. A young man looked up at Spur as he walked in. He looked vaguely familiar but McCoy couldn't quite place the face.

"Can I help you?" the youth asked.

"Yes. I got a dead man outside."

His eyebrows shot up. "A dead man? How—why —I mean, you killed him?"

"That's right. Jack Galde. He's the one that murdered Tex Frank last night."

The boy squirmed. "I see. I didn't know who'd done it. I'm—I'm the new deputy here. Tex deputized me yesterday, on account of how I'm gonna be a married man.''

Then he remembered—the boy who'd challenged Enoch Salt when he accused him of raping his daughter.

''Is Missy Enoch's father still in his cell?'' Spur asked, exhausted.

''Nope. I let him out this morning. He wasn't too happy to see me but he was sure happy to get out.'' The youth peered out the window. ''How'd it happen?''

Spur waved off the question. ''I'll be back to tell you every detail later. But I need some rest now. Hope you understand, Tommy.''

''Sure. I think.''

He jerked his head toward the door. ''You might as well bring him in here.''

''Okay.''

Spur glanced once more at the pudgy man and then headed to his hotel. After hitching his tired horse, he climbed the steps and knocked on the door.

''Patrice?'' he asked.

No answer.

He knocked harder. ''Patrice? You in there?''

The door flew open. A storm of blonde hair rushed out and grasped him in soft, white arms. Patrice Carlon gazed up at him, relieved, her cheeks flushed.

''Spur!'' she said. ''I was hoping it was you.''

He kissed her, right there in the hall, a long, lashing kiss that nearly sent him off his feet.

''Come on.'' He gently pushed the woman back into his hotel room.

She looked at him tentatively. "Did you—I mean, is he—well, did you find Jack Galde?"

Spur nodded. "Not far out of town."

"And is he . . ."

"Yes, Patrice. You won't have to worry about him anymore. He can't hurt you—or anyone—ever again."

She sighed. "Well, that's over." Patrice shook her head. "I still can't believe it all happened to me. Why in the heck did he do it?"

"No way of knowing now." He threw his hat onto the floor and sat on the bed.

"At least you got your job done," she said, going to him. "And saved my life."

He grunted. "Hell, Patrice, I didn't do it all. If you hadn't fought off those two men in the alley, well, I might not have had the opportunity."

She smiled and sat beside him, pressing her thighs to his. "Mother always said I knew how to take care of men. At least, most men."

He folded his hands in his lap and looked down. "So what happens now?"

Patrice lifted his chin. "I've got a few ideas."

He glanced up at her. Lust smouldered in the woman's eyes.

Spur laughed. "I mean *after* that. You planning on staying here and dancing for Mr. Weatherby, going back to Holmes, or returning to St. Louis?"

She shrugged. "Who knows? With Jack out of the way now I guess I could do anything. You know, I haven't even thought about it. All morning long I've just been lying here, worrying about you, wondering if I'd ever see your face—and the rest of you—again."

He nodded. "There may be more Jack Galdes out there."

She stroked his chin and sighed. "I know. But I refuse to think about such horrible possibilities. At least, not now." Patrice touched his chest and ran her fingers along the line of buttons that extended down it.

"I've got a hunch what you *are* thinking about right now," he said as her hand grasped his crotch.

"Mmmmmm."

Her fingers groped, rubbed, explored the bulge between his legs. Spur kissed her forehead and her eyes. "Look, Patrice, I'm just as willing as you— believe me. But maybe we better get a bath." He frowned. "Somehow."

She looked at him, delighted. "That sounds wonderful! And I know just where to go! The Crouching Lion has this incredible bath room. They showed it to me when I checked into my room. It only costs two dollars for two hours and it's all tiled and completely private. Shall we go?"

He removed her hand from his increasingly uncomfortable crotch. "As soon as I can walk."

She chuckled. "The way you talk, Spur!"

Steam hung in the air.

The room was completely covered with the finest gold inlaid tiles that had been imported from Italy. A pile of fluffy white towels sat heaped near an oil lamp which exuded thin golden light. In the center of the room sat the tub—a monstrous, claw-footed affair that could easily hold two or more people.

A sweating boy hauled up one last bucket of fire-warmed water and poured it into the tub. He wiped his forehead and smiled at Patrice.

"There you go, Miss Carlon," he said, grinning at her. "You and your *friend* can take your bath now," he said, surprisingly aware for his age.

"Thank you, Peter. Spur, give the young man a tip, would you?"

He handed the kid a silver dollar.

"Boy oh boy, thanks, mister!" Peter trailed off, bucket dragging along the floor, and banged the door shut.

McCoy locked it and turned to Patrice. She stood by the tub, staring into its steamy contents, looking for all the world like a seer at an ancient Greek oracle.

He moved to her. Tiny droplets of water hung to her blonde hair, flattening it around her face.

"What are you thinking of?" He rubbed her shoulders, feeling her soft skin beneath the thin material.

Patrice shook her head. "Just—just about—"

"Shhhh. The past is just that—the past. Only important thing is *now*."

She glanced up at him and smiled. "Well, heck, I guess you're right. No sense in worrying about the hells we've been through."

They undressed, arms flying, hands gripping, unbuttoning, unstrapping, slipping off, removing. Her dress soon flew on top of Spur's shirt and hat. Boots thudded on the slick floor followed by petticoats and pants. Laughing, they raced to finish before the other.

Soon Spur went to her and gripped her slender

waist. Steam condensed on their bodies as they kissed passionately. When he lifted his head he knew that he was more than ready—throbbingly ready.

She looked down between his legs. "I thought we were going to take a bath, Spur," she chastised with mock despair. "Isn't that why you've dragged me here?"

He grunted. "Okay."

So they washed each other in the stingingly hot water, rubbing away trail dust, cares and worries from their naked bodies. He delighted in his exploration of her, rubbing every square inch of her marble-white flesh as she returned the favor to him. Muscles relaxed as the warm water soothed them.

"Stand up," Patrice said, grinning evilly as she held the huge cake of lye soap.

"Why?"

"You'll see later. Just stand up!"

He rose from the tub. As water sheeted down from his body, Patrice gripped his leg and urged him to turn around. Once he faced away from her the blonde jammed the soap between his buttocks and vigorously scrubbed.

"Hey!" he said.

"Never you mind," she said cheerily as she violated him. "I'm gonna make sure you're really clean."

"Oh . . . . ohhhh . . . kay."

She grabbed his penis and stroked it as she washed, stroked him to full erection.

"Damn it, woman, I don't know if I hate it or love it!" he thundered.

''That's the whole idea,'' she deliciously said.

Spur turned around and splashed down into the tub. ''I think we've had enough of this damned bathing.'' He wriggled the suds from his body.

Her eyes were filled with innocence. ''What've you got in mind?''

''Come on!'' He grabbed her hands and pulled Patrice to her feet.

The naked, dripping couple walked to the pile of towels.

''Now that we're all clean let's get filthy.'' He pushed her down into the towels.

Patrice laughed as he turned to arrange them into a soft bed. She grabbed his hips and licked his left buttock.

''Hey!'' he protested. ''What the hell're you doing?''

''Mmmmmm. Kissing your ass.'' She moved her mouth to his right cheek. Then to the middle.

He shuddered from her unholy actions. ''Where did you get all these crazy ideas, Patrice?'' Spur asked as she licked up and down.

She moaned and removed her head. ''I don't know. I guess it's just the devil in me.''

''I'll put the devil in you—*my* devil. As soon as you—oh! Oh! Oh hell! You stop that, girl, you hear? You just stop that—ohhhh! Dammit, that feels goodd!''

''Mmmmmmm.''

She moved between his legs, licking down to his hanging scrotum, sucking it into her moist mouth, humming and probing his fullness with her tongue.

Spur shook as she squirmed and turned around, sliding her mouth up from his testicles to the root of his erection. She licked up it, pressing her lips around his shaft until she'd met its pulsing head. Patrice enmouthed him in liquid fire.

"Ahhh! Damn, that's fine, Patrice! Don't stop now!"

She slid her lips up and down along it, savoring it, staring into his steamy eyes as she pleasured him. Spur laid his hands on her shoulders as erotic sensations rocketed through him.

"Jeez!" He bent forward slightly and grasped her breasts, cupped them, squeezed them softly while thrusting into her mouth. Patrice groaned and quickened her pace, accepting his pumps, opening her throat.

Steam enveloped their bodies. All too soon Spur felt himself getting dangerously close. Patrice sensed it and released him.

"Now," she said, flopping down onto the towels. "Now I want you to do it." She pressed the backs of her hands against her thighs and stroked upward. "Do it to me, Spur. Put it in. Fill me up and make me feel like a woman!"

He got into position and rubbed his penis against her opening. "You've got me so worked up I don't know how long I'll be good for."

"I don't care!" The woman bumped her crotch against him, urging him to impale her. "Just stick it in!" Her gaze burned into his through the mist laden air.

He pushed into her, sliding, driving. Patrice came alive. She met his thrust, slamming him full-length into her. She groaned and squeezed her eyes in temporary pain before opening them wide and looking up at him.

"Oh yeah. Oh yes, Spur! Heck, you're gonna spoil me for any other man. But I don't care. I don't! Just fuck me. Fuck me! Fuck my pussy!"

He obliged, pulled out and pounded back into her. Their slick bodies joined, separated, joined as they worked out their mutual lusts. Spur felt strong and alive as he rocked in and out. They established a rhythm of slow thrusts and quick withdrawals that increased in speed with each push. Soon their bodies banged together and Patrice groaned and moaned beneath him.

"Faster. Open me up. Oh god oh god oh god!"

McCoy revelled in the pleasure that shot through him, surging through every part of his being, spinning his mind until all he was aware of was Patrice and their warm connection and her willingness to give her body to him.

He rode her harder until his testicles banged against her crotch. The blonde woman shook and shuddered, dug her fingernails into his back and thrashed her head from side to side as the pleasure built within her and mounted to an unbearable, undeniable peak.

"Yes! Yes! Yes Spur!" she said, rolling through her orgasm and clutching his body with unshamed lust as she shivered and bucked beneath him.

McCoy deepened his thrusts, puffing out his breath in short blasts, staring down at the climaxing woman, driving himself closer and closer until he couldn't hold back, couldn't stop the ultimate release that boiled up within him.

"Patrice!"

He yelled and pumped and exploded. A thousand stars wheeled before his eyes as he slammed into

her, grunting and snorting and gripping her
shoulders as every muscle in his body tensed and
celebrated his orgasm. Lightning raced through
him with each spurt, electrifying him, empowering
him with the primal savagery of pure lust.

It finally ended. The incredible feelings washed
through him to be replaced with sweet lethargy.
He halted his thrusts and lay panting on top of her
as their genitals clung to each other.

Spur closed his eyes and gasped. His breath shot
against a curl of blonde hair, sending it flying into
the air as he desperately tried to recover his senses.

Below him, Patrice sighed and grabbed him and
held the spent man like she'd never let go.

It was some time later that Spur realized he was
crushing the woman. He gripped her hip and rolled
Patrice on top of him.

The woman kissed his nose. "Fun, wasn't it?"
she asked with shining eyes.

He nodded.

"I thought so." She laid her cheek on his hairy
chest. "But don't you think it's time we had a
bath?"

Spur met her at the train station in Fagan. He'd
ridden back to Holmes, paid her bill and rescued
her belongings from her hotel room. He piled the
leather bags at her feet.

Patrice was dazzling in the full sunlight, her
blonde hair glowing beneath the white hat, her
luscious body wrapped in a matching silk dress
trimmed with white lace and real pearl buttons.

The woman was relieved to see him. "Just in